THE WIND BOY

The Wind Boy

by

Ethel Cook Eliot

Illustrated by Sylvia Thomas

Raven Rocks Press

1996

ISBN 0-9615961-4-7
Library of Congress Catalog Card Number
96-67921

Calligraphy by Sharon Hanse
Composition by Raven Rocks Press
Text set in Berthold Garamond
Printed by Patterson Printing
Recycled paper

The Wind Boy may be ordered from:
Raven Rocks Press
53650 Belmont Ridge, Beallsville, OH 43716
740-926-1481

TO

MY LITTLE GIRL

Torka

WHO, IF ANYTHING NEEDS EXPLAINING,

KNOWS MORE ABOUT IT THAN I DO

Publisher's Preface

First published in 1923, *The Wind Boy* was slightly revised by the author for the 1945 edition.

In this third edition we have chosen to keep the author's wording and capitalization, for the most part, even though some words will be unfamiliar to many readers today.

The publisher's family and the artist, Sylvia Thomas, have loved this story for many years. We hope you will enjoy it as we do.

John M. Morgan

Contents

	About the Author	11
1	The Girl From the Mountains	15
2	The Robe of Starry Brightness	26
3	Shopping With Nan	40
4	Kay and Gentian are Measured	50
5	The Keepsake	62
6	Noon in the Tulip Garden	75
7	The Spring in the Woods	89
8	Through Music	98
9	The Other School	109
10	The Secret Door	121
11	Gentian at the Loom	133
12	On Paths of Night	148
13	Kay and the Masker	159
14	Nan and the Policeman	171
15	Rosemarie is Waked by the Little Silver Bell	183
16	Rosemarie Comes to School	198
17	Detra Meets the Artist	212
18	Comrades	222

ETHEL COOK ELIOT
1890-1972

Ethel Cook was one of six children born to Cornelius Cook, a Protestant minister, and his wife Carrie, in upper New York State. Her childhood was spent in beautiful country, "low living and high thinking," as the saying goes. The minister was sometimes paid in potatoes.

When church authorities informed Cornelius that he would have to preach doctrine in which he did not believe, he left the church, moved to Pittsfield, Massachusetts, and sold life insurance. This traumatic change rescued the family finances. All the discussion Ethel must have heard about theological matters deeply colored her young mind. Early mystical experiences and an Irish live-in grandmother's stories colored Ethel's mind yet more deeply. The most impressive experience she remembered was watching a fairy slide down the porch banister, not once, but over and over, on a rainy day. All five living children saw it from the window of the tiny, cramped living room.

Ethel began writing stories as soon as she could read. In high school she was accused of copying an essay the teacher could not believe she had written. After high school she found writing and editorial work with *Ladies' World* magazine in New York City, and sold fairy stories to *Story Tellers* magazine. Through her writing she met and married Samuel Atkins Eliot, Jr., a grandson of Harvard president, Charles William Eliot. Samuel soon joined the faculty of

Smith College in Northampton, Massachusetts, where the couple spent their life.

While raising two daughters and a son, Ethel wrote more than a dozen books, that fall in three periods. The first, written in her twenties, are arguably her finest works—a series of children's fantasies, although she never called them that. She felt that these works were realistic in a high sense, and called them "imaginative writing." The most successful of these is *The Wind Boy*, which still evokes enthusiasm from people with a hunger for mystical experience. Other books from Ethel's first period include: *The House On the Edge of Things*, *The Little House in the Fairy Wood*, *The House Above the Trees*, and *Buttercup Days*. Like many of the best children's books, Ethel's books speak to children on one level and are appreciated by adults on another.

In 1925, after an earnest spiritual search, Ethel became a Catholic. Then began her second period, in which she wrote merry mystery stories for teenage girls. Her third period involved adult novels with Catholic themes and characters. But Ethel is best remembered today for her early children's books, in which she expressed her own instinctive and experiential wisdom.

–Anne Eliot Crompton
1996

THE WIND BOY

Chapter 1

The Girl from the Mountains

IN a spring twilight a young girl was walking down a village street. Just at a glance anyone might know she was a stranger there. For one thing her dress was like nobody else's. It was the color of sunlight on a brown forest path when the sun is low behind the trees; and it was made tunic fashion with a belt of twisted grasses. Under the tunic was a white guimpe of sheerest, softest lawn gathered at the neck and wrists with a silver cord. To add to the strangeness, she wore on her feet sandals that looked as though she had made them herself out of bark and braided weeds. In one hand she swung a loosely tied bundle wrapped in purple. Her head was hatless, and though she was a tall girl, quite grown up, her hair was blowing free in soft curls almost to her shoulders, the color of a forest brook when the sun finds it. Do you wonder that people turned to look after her?

But the strange girl never noticed the surprised glances of the villagers, or the cries of the children. She walked along, her head up, her clear eyes eager; for she had an errand in this village that made her feet step lightly, and lighted her face with an expectant smile.

She walked along quickly and smiling until, almost at the edge of the village, she came to a white mansion, bowered in gardens, and looking as out of place in its setting as she herself looked, only in a different way. There she paused—as who came to the village ever failed to pause—to look up at the mansion's graceful arches and vine-covered walls.

"And well she may stare!" thought the village Policeman who was coming toward her along the street. "She looks countrified enough never to have seen such a house as that one."

The strange girl spoke to the Policeman just as he was about to pass her.

"Can you tell me, please, who lives in that house?" she asked.

The Policeman stopped, rather glad of an opportunity to awe the country girl.

"Yes, I can tell you. A very famous Artist lives there. He's rich, too. You may have read about him in the papers."

"It's a nice house," the strange girl said. "I like it like that—so tall and white, with the tree shadows on it."

The Policeman didn't want to hurt her feelings, but he couldn't help laughing.

"Tree shadows! My eye! Why, the architect the Artist got to draw the plans is as famous as the Artist. People come from all over just to look at that house, and those gardens off at the back, too. They run down almost to the woods—gardens and lawns and terraces. A little later in the summer those gardens are a marvel. Better than a flower show."

"It looks a good place for children to play. There's as much lawn as there is garden. Was it planned for the children?"

"No. Well, for one child, a little perhaps. His little granddaughter. She's a lonely little thing. She mostly plays alone."

"Why?" asked the strange girl, surprised.

"That's just the way it is. How do I know why? Snobbery, perhaps. Or fear. She's all the Artist has left in his family, and he's overcareful of her. You're from the country, aren't you?"

"Yes, I am from the country," said the strange girl. "I'm from the mountains."

As the strange girl said this, for the first time the Policeman's eyes met and looked directly into the girl's eyes. And at that instant something odd happened to him. He thought that here, at the end of Main Street, he was standing all by himself on the pavement and holding conversation with the purple mountains that lifted their heads, far off, above the roofs of the Artist's mansion. But he was not alone, of course; for here was the country girl in her brown tunic and funny sandals. And he was looking straight into her eyes. It must have been in her eyes he saw the mountains. The notion went as quickly as it had come.

"But who lives in that tiny house?" asked the strange girl. She had turned away her eyes.

"That? That little brown cottage? Foreigners. Refugees. A mother and her two children. The father went away to the war and then they were driven out of their own village and country by the enemy. They came here and the mother got factory work in the city."

"That is the house I am looking for, I think," said the strange girl. "I am answering the mother's advertisement for a general housework girl. See, here it is." She pulled out of her pocket a clipping that read:

"Wanted: a girl for general housework, who can do plain cooking and likes children. Small wages, but a good home."

"Small wages! I should think so!" laughed the Policeman. "Much good it'll do you to answer that ad. Why, the woman hardly earns enough to feed themselves—and wants to hire a cook. That's refugees for you! They don't make sense."

"The ad makes sense, though, and I've come a long way to answer it."

As the strange girl passed him to go to the little brown house, again the Policeman saw distant, purple mountains in her eyes. He stayed for some time looking after her, wondering at himself.

The little brown cottage stood in a tiny garden with a tall, thick hedge of lilac bushes between it and the Artist's lawn. The strange girl crossed the street and went in at the low swinging gate. The door was around at the side of the house, and to get to it the strange girl had to pass the open sitting-room windows. She stopped to look in.

It was a little, low, oblong sitting room she saw, with

thin golden-brown curtains at the windows, and golden brown cushions on the chairs. There was very little furniture, and what there was was worn and rickety. But it was a happy room for all of that. There was a shelf of books on the wall, and under it a square table with a bowl of bright tulips, purple, red and white, in the middle of it.

In a minute, as the strange girl stood there, a little girl and boy came in from the kitchen, carrying spoons and plates to set on the table for supper.

The little girl was eight years old and her brother was nine. You could see easily enough that they were foreigners. In that village, even in that country, there was no such copper-colored hair. The boy's head was a thick mop of burnished copper. The girl's hair was copper-colored too, and soft as cobwebs. It was braided in two smooth pigtails that ended just half-way down her back. Both were dressed in dull blue flannel that looked as though it had once been the same piece. And, indeed, this was true, for last year, when they were living at home in their own village, it had been one of their mother's prettiest dresses.

The little girl was smiling, as at some secret, happy thought.

"Oh, Kay," she said, softly, suddenly, as they were putting the things about on the table, "let's not wait for Mother to make the porridge. Her train's so late! I'm sure I can manage perfectly. I've watched her so many times!"

"Of course you could manage. So could I. But Mother doesn't want us to light the stove. You know that as well as I do."

"Oh, but if it were to surprise her? She does come home so tired! And to find a nice hot supper?"

But Kay shook his head. "I'm sure it would make her tireder if we did what she's told us not to do."

The little girl's face fell. The strange girl, leaning in at the open window, heard her sigh.

"Oh, don't sigh, little copper-haired girl," she suddenly cried. "I am quite old, almost grown up, you see. So I can light the fire. And we *will* surprise your mother!"

Both children turned in amazement toward the window. And the strange girl leaning there saw something beside amazement in their faces. It was fear.

"Why should they be frightened by a friendly voice?" she wondered.

Of course the minute they saw her smiling eyes their fear vanished.

"Oh, will you?" cried the little girl.

But Kay asked, "Who are you?"

"My name is Nan. And I have come all the way from the mountains answering your mother's advertisement for a general housework girl. But perhaps she has found one?"

"No. No one has even come to talk to her about it. You see they all know how poor we are."

"Then may I come in, please? And we will get supper to surprise her."

The little girl, standing wide-eyed and eager behind her brother, now cried, "Oh, splendid! Do, do come in. I'll open the door," and she started quickly toward it.

But Nan, the stranger girl, laughed and, putting one hand against the window casing, leapt lightly over the sill into the room. That surprised the children. Why, Kay himself who was strong and supple could never have done that. But Nan had done it as though it were nothing!

"You are Kay," she said to the boy, "for I heard her call you that. But what is your name?" she asked the little girl.

"Gentian."

"Gentian! That is a flower." Nan bent down and looked into the eager upturned face in the twilight of the room.

"And you are *like* a gentian. Have you ever seen one?"

"No, we haven't." Kay answered for his sister. "But Father has—in a country where he traveled once. They are blue like Gentian's eyes, and though they grow among stones on windy hillsides, they are quiet like the sky. Father always said that one small gentian had all the sky folded around in its soft fringes. It is a special magic that makes that possible. Gentian magic. Cold and frost do not scare it for it has the whole sky held close to give it company and heart."

"Yes," said Nan. "The gentian is like that. Are you like that?" she asked the little girl.

But Gentian laughed. "The cold scares me," she said. "Last winter it was dreadful. That was before Mother got work in the factory and could buy us warm coats. Then—"

Kay interrupted. "Father says she's like that."

But Gentian did not listen. "Let's get supper," she cried. "How glad I am you're here, Nan! Mother will be so surprised!"

When the stove was lighted in the kitchen, and the kettle put on to boil, Kay suddenly said, "It's queer to have you so friendly, Nan, and not laughing at us at all. Everyone else here in this country seems to be laughing. It's because we're foreigners, I suppose. Once I told a boy at school about Gentian's name and what it means. He laughed and laughed. I'm careful now not to say the things I think to anybody."

"But you say the things you think to me. You began right at once to say them. How was that?"

Kay looked at her, wondering himself. "You're different from anybody I've ever seen before," he said then. "I forget that you're a stranger."

Nan still looked at him. And then his eyes suddenly wavered from those clear, quiet ones that were so kind. He bent his head and turned away. You must not like him any the less when I tell you that he had turned away to hide his tears. They were strange happy tears. How splendid to have a friend, and all so suddenly, in this alien village!

When the porridge was made and a salad to go with it, Nan and the two children went back into the sitting room to wait for Mother. It was almost dark now, but they did not light the lamp or the candles. They sat on a bench under the window, Nan in the middle; and she began to tell them stories that she had learned in the mountains.

But she had hardly begun when there came a rustle and a scratching—odd little sounds—at the window above their heads. Both children sprang up and faced about. But Nan only turned her head. There, dim in the falling darkness, was the weirdest face. Little green eyes, a huge nose, terribly frowning brows and pointed brown ears! It was enough to frighten anybody.

The children backed away toward the other side of the room, silently terrified. But Nan, to their amazed horror, made a grab toward the face. It ducked away just in time and vanished from the window. The children heard its feet running lightly away around Kay's flower beds in the garden.

Then Kay cried, "It never came right up to our window before!"

Gentian ran to Nan and hid her face against her breast. "It *was* an ugly face," Nan comforted. "But it's only a mask somebody has put on to frighten you. Anyone can see that. Who is it?"

"Yes, it is a mask," Kay agreed. "I was the first of all the children to know that. They don't believe me yet about it. But it's just as scary for all its being only a mask!"

"I don't see how," Nan said sensibly. "Who wears it?"

"Why, that's the scary part. *Nobody can find out.*"

"Well, it looked to me as though it was a child, some little mischief or other," Nan said.

"No, it can't be."

"Why can't it be?"

"Because if it was any child in the village it would have been caught before now. It has been frightening children for days. One very little boy when he saw it on the street in the dusk was made sick. Our teacher, and the Artist who lives next door, and even the Policeman himself say it must be caught and when it is caught, punished. But I think even the Policeman is a little afraid of it!"

"Where do the children see it, usually?"

"It's always on this street, in front of our house or the Artist's. And it's always just at twilight. It never came into our yard before, though, and right up at the window."

"And it hadn't better do so again," Nan said soberly, "unless it wants to get caught. Frightening people isn't any way to have fun!"

She walked suddenly back to the window and leaned out of it.

"The ugly thing is not in the garden," she said. "Let's

just forget it until it comes again. Then we'll *catch it,* and pull off its mask. But there's someone at the gate. She's coming up the path."

That was Detra, of course, the children's mother. They rushed to the door to meet her.

Chapter 2

The Robe of Starry-Brightness

DETRA was surprised enough to find the strange girl
from the mountains waiting for her in her house. But
the children would not let Nan explain. They were wild
with happy excitement. It was like the old days back in their
own village when it was Hazar, their father, who went out
to work, and Detra stayed at home with her children. They
often greeted him with surprises.

"Oh, Mother, we have such a surprise! Shut your eyes.
Say not a word!"

Detra sat down on the bench under the window. Her
train had been late and so crowded that she had stood in it
all the way from the city. She was very tired, and glad to
shut her eyes. But when she had done so, it was as though
a light had gone out in the room, for Detra's eyes were so
bright with mother love, the children missed them when
they were shut.

Then Kay and Gentian and Nan on tiptoes hurried into
the kitchen and brought in the supper. When they had

brought it in, and Nan had lighted the lamp and the three candles, that stood on the bookshelf, and set the bowl of tulips exactly in the middle of the table, the children both cried at once, "Now you may look, Mother darling! Look!"

And when the tired mother opened her eyes and saw the warm food, nicely cooked, and the flowers and the candles and the children's shining faces, she was as surprised and as happy as they could have hoped.

But she looked at Nan in a very puzzled way.

"Who are you?" she asked. "You have been very kind to my children and to me. You do not live in this village?"

"I have just today come from the mountains," said Nan. "I am answering your advertisement for a general housework girl. I hope I'll do."

Detra's first surprise was as nothing to her surprise now. But she was silent for a minute.

"Oh, she will do! She will, Mother," cried Kay and Gentian in one breath. "You will let her stay?"

Detra passed her hand across her eyes. "I am not dreaming?" she asked.

At that, how the children laughed! "Asleep? Not you. Why, Mother, you are as wide awake as we. And she may stay?"

All this time Nan stood there looking as eager and hopeful as the children. Her face, her eyes, her half-grave smile all said, "Yes, may I stay?"

At last Detra spoke, looking up wonderingly at the strange girl. "But I can't pay you! Not what you're worth!

Why, you aren't the sort of maid I had in mind at all. You are—You are a superior person somehow!"

At that Nan shook her head. "No, I am just a girl from the mountains," she said. "I am sure you can pay me all I need."

"And you are so young!" said Detra then. "How old are you? Fifteen? Sixteen?"

"Back in the mountains we do not reckon our age. I do not know how old I am. But I know that I am old enough to do plain cooking and keep a house clean, and look after the children. I have come a long way, Detra, to answer your advertisement."

Detra did not at that moment think it strange that Nan should call her by her Christian name. She only remembered to wonder at it later.

"I shall be very happy to have you stay," she said, "if only you are sure you really want to. You see, it is not just the small wages I can pay. It is also that we do not have many nice things to eat. Will you be contented with almost nothing but soups and salads? Cakes and sweets we seldom have, for I am quite poor."

The children were holding their breath. Suppose, oh suppose this new, gay, beautiful friend should go away to a house where there were better things to eat and more wages—to a fine place like the Artist's over the hedge! Their mother might have heard their thoughts, for she added, "The Artist who lives in the beautiful mansion across the hedge could very probably make a place for you. His housekeeper is always engaging new maids and discharging old ones."

But the children threw themselves upon her. "You are going to stay and live with us and be with us forever!" they cried. "Mother really means that. Don't listen to anything else."

"Bring another plate and cup, then," said Detra. "The table is set for three only."

"I have set a place for myself in the kitchen," Nan answered. "You have your children only at night. I shall be happy with them much of the day. Is there anything else you need?"

Detra looked at the table carefully. "No, you have thought of everything. Have you plenty for yourself?"

"Yes, thank you."

Then Nan went out, softly closing the door into the kitchen.

The supper was delicious. Not even back in their home town had food tasted any better. How grateful Detra was to have found such a meal ready and perfect for her! Always before, when she got home from the factory, no matter how tired she was, she had had to prepare supper herself.

While they ate, the children told their mother all about the coming of Nan: how she had jumped in over the sill, and how she had frightened away the Masker that had come right up to their very window and stood looking in. "She wasn't a bit afraid! She just grabbed at the mask and almost caught it!"

But at the recounting of this adventure Detra was troubled. "The Masker in our garden!" she exclaimed. "Oh, why doesn't the Policeman or someone catch it! It is wicked to frighten children so. I should think the Artist would do something! He himself has a little girl to be frightened!"

She was really talking to herself, but the children heard.

"Oh, no," Gentian said. "Rosemarie will never be frightened. Her nurse and her governess are always with her. The Masker would keep away from them. And at night she sleeps in her high nursery up above the treetops. A big girl like that to sleep in a nursery! But she will not be frightened."

"Oh, I hope she is never frightened," Kay said almost under his breath. For Kay, although he had never even spoken to the Artist's little granddaughter, felt that he knew her and liked her very much. When he caught glimpses of her from the car in which she went riding in the charge of her governess, or times when she looked down at him from her high nursery window when he had reached the top of the cherry tree in their garden, her merry brown eyes seemed always to be saying the same thing: "I like you, ever so much. If only we were allowed, we might be such splendid playmates. I have read so many exciting stories that I want to tell you. I like sea stories best, stories of pirates and runaway boys and hidden treasure. You do, too, I know. And I want you to let me climb your cherry tree. You are splendid at tree climbing. Yesterday I thought you were falling, but you caught yourself. Oh, I do want to play with you!"

How even such merry brown eyes as Rosemarie's were could say all that in a passing flash I do not know. But Kay was always sure they did. And afterwards Rosemarie said he was right; she *was* thinking all that, and much more.

So now he repeated in a whisper, "Oh, I hope she is never frightened!"

"Well, I don't want her to be frightened, either," Detra answered, for she had heard. "But just because his own little granddaughter is safe is no reason why the Artist should go on letting all the other little boys and girls in the village be frightened. It is always on this street, near his house. He could do something."

"But he has done something," Kay assured her. "In school today Miss Todd told us that the Artist had promised that the Masker was to be caught and no child frightened by it any more. He is going to give the Policeman a lot of money when he catches it. And then the Masker is to be punished. Miss Todd warned us in case it might be one of us. Imagine!"

Detra sighed. "I am glad that something is being done. They know then what a shame it is to let children be frightened."

At that minute Nan came in to clear the table.

The children helped her, moving back and forth with her from the sitting room to the kitchen. When all was cleared, the floor brushed, and the table set back against the wall, they went into the kitchen to do the dishes.

"Leave the door open," Detra called. "I like to hear your voices."

Then she went up to her room and soon came down with something in her hands. Nan, standing at the sink, could see through the open doorway that it was a little statuette made of plastilina. Detra set it on the table under the lamp and, drawing up a chair, began to work on it with her fingers and a little tool, sharp at one end, blunt at the other.

"That is the Wind Boy," Kay confided. "Mother is an artist." He said it proudly.

Detra heard, and looked up to smile at him. "It may be the Wind Boy sometime," she said a little wistfully. "I am sure he is lighter and freer and more joyous than I have made him though—ever so much so, the real Wind Boy. He should be as happy and as light as air. But somehow, he won't come right!"

Then to herself she added softly, "I am too tired, perhaps, at night after the day's work. I might make him right in the morning. But this is the only time I have."

Nan had left the dishes and drawn near. She stood above Detra, looking down at the little figure.

The Wind Boy was not like any human boy that you have ever seen. His hair grew in thick, soft curls over his head. His eyes were far apart, wide, and should have been happy, but somehow they were touched with sadness. His dress was a fluttering tunic not quite to his knees and his body was slim and supple. High above his head were spread wide, strong, swift wings. His feet were just leaving the earth in flight, and his face seemed to say, "Yes, I am coming!"

Yes, all this was true of the Wind Boy even if he was just a little statuette of plastilina! It was a very beautiful little statuette. But even though it was so beautiful and wonderful Detra, and even the children, knew that it could become ever so much more beautiful.

"Why isn't he happier, Mother?" asked Kay, who had drawn near, too. "If I could fly, I'd be happier than that."

"If I could fly," Gentian said softly, "I'd fly with more of me—WITH ALL OF ME!"

"I don't know," puzzled Detra, passing her hands across her eyes. "I wish I *could* make him happier, and make *all of him* ready to fly!"

But Nan said nothing, though she bent down and looked for a long time earnestly and with great interest at the Wind Boy. After a time she went back to her dishes.

"Mother may show the Wind Boy to the Artist, if it ever comes as she wants it," Kay told her as he wiped the last spoon and handed it to Gentian to put away. "But she doesn't want anyone to speak of that yet. It is a secret."

"But if it is a secret, why do you tell me?" asked Nan.

"Oh, but somehow—I didn't think—not to you!"

What Kay meant was that Nan was already so dear to him and Gentian that for a minute he did not remember that she was not one of them.

But Detra had heard from the next room. And now she lifted her eyes from her work on the Wind Boy to say, "Don't bother, Kay, this time. You didn't mean to let my secret out, I know. And Nan will remember not to tell. It is just the village people. We don't want them to laugh at us, that is all."

"But why should they laugh?" asked Nan.

"I don't know," Detra answered. "But they do, all the time. Our ways are not their ways, I suppose."

Just then Nan noticed that Gentian's eyes were beginning to droop. "Let us go to bed, and leave the house quiet for your mother to try to get the Wind Boy right," she suggested.

"Yes, do go to bed, children dear," agreed Detra. "Tomorrow is Saturday and you will want to play hard. And Gentian, you may show Nan her room in the attic. I am sorry that it isn't a nicer one.

But when Gentian and Kay too had taken Nan up to the attic room, she thought it was very nice indeed. You will think so too.

But first I must tell you about this little brown house that was set down like a stepping stone to the Artist's magnificent one. Downstairs there were only the kitchen and the sitting room and a little hall, upstairs Detra's and Gentian's room, and back of that Kay's room, and above these two rooms, the attic, a long, low room with a slanting, plastered ceiling, and a dormer window at each end, with their sills almost on a level with the floor. Under one sloping side stood a narrow bed, painted white. By one of the windows was a chest of drawers, and in front of the other window a low, three-legged stool. By the bed lay a strip of faded blue rug. That was all there was in the room!

But when Nan had put the candle on the top of the chest of drawers, the light gleamed pleasantly on the white walls and ceiling, and the faded blue rug by the bed shone like a bit of dim water.

Kay had carried up Nan's bundle, wrapped carelessly in its purple covering. It was very small, he thought, to hold all of Nan's wardrobe. Why, most people who went anywhere to stay took a trunk along at least! He laid the bundle on the white coverlet of the bed.

"What a beautiful room!" exclaimed Nan, looking all around.

And Gentian and Kay did see suddenly that it was a very beautiful room. How it happened I don't know. Perhaps it was so beautiful because the night had got in through the windows, which were both open. The room now was beautiful, like the spring evening, only that it was smaller. The spring night air, sweet with the smell of budding cherry blossoms, and spring flowers and grass and earth stirred against their faces, and Gentian thought, "It is just as though we were out in some little room in the sky and all the spring fragrance coming up to us there!"

Then she noticed the purple bundle that Kay had put on the bed. "Oh, may we see into your bundle?" she begged.

Perhaps it was rude to ask that, but Gentian did not mean to be rude; nor Kay when he echoed, "Oh, yes, do let us see what you brought."

Nan laughed. "Little curiosities! Yes, you may undo it, Gentian; it is my clothes."

So Gentian with eager fingers undid the knotted purple cloth and, opening it on the bed, spread out Nan's things.

There was another dress, wood-brown just like the one Nan was wearing. There was another guimpe, too, sheer,

soft and white, gathered with silver strings at the neck and
wrists. There was a change of underlinen, very white and
soft too. And there was a nightgown.

But Gentian did not know that it was a nightgown. Nor
would you. It was the color of the spring night sky, faint
blue; and it was scattered through and through with glimmering stars. The stars were not embroidered on the cloth
or woven there, but seemed to shine forth from deep
within it, just as the stars show forth in the sky. And though
at first glance the robe was only a film, still it was dense, and
you could look deeply into it as into the sky. When Gentian took it up to spread it out on the bed, the scent of
pines and fir trees and sap and arbutus hung in the air all
about her; and she had to look to see that she had anything

in her hands at all, for the robe had no weight. For a minute Gentian thought that a strip of the sky must somehow have blown into the window and onto the bed.

"What is this?" she asked, wonderingly. "It is too beautiful for a dress."

"Yes, it is too beautiful for a day dress when there is work to be done," answered Nan. "It is my nightrobe."

"Do you wear it to *sleep in*?" cried Gentian, amazed, for it was hard to believe that anyone would put on anything so lovely just to go to bed in.

"Yes, I sleep in it."

"But I never heard of such a nightgown."

"Back in the mountains we always wear nightgowns like this."

"But why is it so light? When I pick it up it's just as though it were winds that lifted out of my hands, and if I *held*, might carry me away with them."

"Yes, that is what I feel too, when I wear it," said Nan.

Nan was sitting cross-legged on the floor by the low window sill, her elbows on her knees, her chin in her hands. Her eyes were grave and thoughtful.

"I am wondering about the Wind Boy," she said. "Why should a Wind Boy be sad?"

"Why, just because Mother hasn't managed to get him happier," answered Kay. "He isn't real, you know. He's just a statue." He added these sensible words because Nan was looking so strangely serious about it.

"Yes, the little image down there isn't alive, of course,"

she agreed, looking up at Kay. "But I am wondering about the Wind Boy himself. I don't like to think that he is sad. A Wind Boy should not be sad."

Even Gentian laughed at that. "Why, there isn't any real Wind Boy," Kay said. "Mother just made him up, you know—because she's an artist and can."

But Nan stayed grave. "That's just why there *is* a real Wind Boy," she said. "Because your mother *is* an artist, a true one. If she weren't an artist, but just a pretend one, well, then there very likely wouldn't be any Wind Boy. But don't you yourselves know that since she has made him so true, there must be a *truer* one, if we could only see him?"

No, the children did not know that. But Nan looked so wisely kind and beautifully grave there in the open window by starlight and candlelight that they believed now what they could not understand at all.

"Do you suppose he is down there in the garden, perhaps, looking in at your mother as she works?" Nan wondered. "It's not right that he should be sad, wherever he is!"

"When he can fly too!" cried Kay, who for this minute believed in the Wind Boy. "How could a boy that could fly be sad?"

"Let's find out," said Nan then softly. "If we can find out, perhaps we can help him to be glad again."

"And if we can make him glad again we shall be helping Mother too," cried Kay, his eyes bright at the thought. "For she would have a happy Wind Boy to copy then, and get him right, the way she thinks he ought to be!"

Gentian and Kay both knelt by Nan and looked down into the garden. But though they looked so hard that they almost saw the color of the jonquils in the starlight, they saw no Wind Boy, wandering troubled and alone.

"We will find him somehow, though," Nan promised. "For he is here, somewhere near, or how came that little image! Only now, tonight, we had better sleep, as she told us to."

A little later, when Kay was fast asleep in his room and Gentian was about to fall asleep in her bed in her mother's room, she suddenly said to herself, "Oh I wish I might give the Wind Boy some of my happiness! I have so much and to spare! I am brimmed full—like the spring we found in the woods with Mother last Sunday! Nan makes my happiness, because she is here. She is up there, just above me in her starry-brightness." (That is what Gentian that night and always after called the blue nightrobe.) "Perhaps she will float far tonight, it is so light, that gown—but she will come back before morning. Together we three shall find the Wind Boy— He will be happy again—the statue will come right— Mother will be happy— The spring was brimmed full of the most sparkling——"

But in the midst of these dreamy thoughts, Gentian forgot everything and floated off like a petal into sleep.

Chapter 3

Shopping with Nan

THE next morning the children woke so late that Detra had already gone to her work. Their first thought was of Nan. Would she still be there? Or was last night just a dream made up by their lonely hearts? When they remembered the starry-brightness nightrobe, they thought it might very well be a dream.

But no. When they got downstairs, there she was, busy with soap and clean white cloths washing the kitchen windows! And their breakfast was waiting for them in the sitting room on the table by the tulip bowl. The Wind Boy was on the table too, just in front of Gentian's place, for Detra had been too tired to put him away last night, and in the morning she never had time for anything.

"You see, Mother tried to make him smile last night," said Kay, looking closely at the little figure. "See, she turned his mouth up at the corners. But it's not quite a real smile. It's more as if he was pretending to be happy."

"Something still bothers him," Gentian said quietly.

"It's just as Nan said. Oh, if only we could find out, and help him!"

Kay looked at his sister doubtfully. But Gentian looked steadily back. Somehow during last night's sleep, she had become sure for herself about the Wind Boy, and did not just have to take Nan's word for him any more. He must be real and not far off. How else could Mother have found out about him at all?

But as Kay wondered, there came a sudden loud knock at the door. It was so loud and so unexpected that it made the children jump. No one but the milkman and the grocer came to the door of the little brown house in the morning. And the milkman had already been, for here was the good cream on their cereal. And the grocer never got around so early.

Before they could remember to jump up and answer the surprising knock, Nan had come in from the kitchen and gone to the door. The children heard her say "Good morning, Officer. Is there something—?"

Then they heard the Policeman interrupting, harshly. "Yes, there is something. Those two rascally children! Which of 'em is it? I've come to find out."

At the Policeman's rough, sudden words Nan had backed away from him, and he stepped into the hall, and now almost pushed her into the sitting room where the children sat, frozen, listening.

Nan looked at the children over her shoulder, and their wide eyes and frightened faces made her straighten up and

face the Policeman, refusing to let him come one step farther. And although she was just a girl, with short curls to
her neck, she seemed very tall and protecting to the children back in the room.

"What do you mean? What do you want?" she asked
the Policeman in a cool, clear voice.

"What I want is to know which one of 'em's doing this
funny business with the mask. For one of 'em it must be.
I'm on the right track at last."

"I'm glad if you are really on the right track," Nan said
then. "It's horrid and a shame to frighten children. Whom
do you suspect?"

"Suspect? I *know!*"

"Well, who?"

"One of those youngsters over there." He nodded his
head toward the children.

Kay's heart sank with doubt of what might happen, and
Gentian trembled; for the Policeman had always filled them
with awe and a little anxiety, even though they had done
nothing wrong. And now to have him in the very room with
them, nodding toward them and calling them rascally—well,
it was pretty terrible!

But Nan stayed calm. "No, no. You have made a mistake,"
she said. "The Masker did come and look in at our window last
night. I was sitting here, over there on that bench with the children, telling them stories. It looked right in at the window by
our heads. I tried to catch it, but it ducked and ran. So you see
it couldn't have been either Kay or Gentian."

The Policeman looked at Nan as she spoke, and she looked steadily back at him. But as he looked he forgot all about Nan. He thought he was standing on a mountain trail. Underfoot pine needles lay golden in sunlight. The purple mountain was over him. He believed what the wind said, and the stream near by, and the murmuring branches. No one doubts those voices. And what was it they were saying?– "You see, it couldn't have been Kay or Gentian."

The dream lasted but a second, if it were a dream, and there was Nan again. Her voice was like the voices of the mountain; you could not doubt what it said.

"It's strange," he apologized, beginning to back out into the hall. "But you yourself said it did come in here and right up to the window. I watched it that far. It came stealing through the hole in the lilac hedge. I didn't stop to open the gate but jumped it. I tripped though and got a tumble, losing sight of the Masker. I didn't see it again, although I went all around your house. Then I thought it must have gone back through the hole in the hedge and I went into the Artist's ground to search. That took a long time and there was nothing there. Then I made up my mind the Masker must have got into this house. Then it came to me it was one of these children.

"But by that time it was long after dark, and I thought you must all be asleep, except the mother, whom I saw through the window working on a sort of statue. I hadn't a mind to disturb her, she looked so tired. And anyhow, she wasn't the Masker—I could see that. *She* would never frighten children."

"No, and *you* wouldn't either," Nan said, glancing toward Kay and Gentian and then back to the Policeman.

"No, you're right. I wouldn't," he agreed. "Sorry I bothered you." And he went out of the door. The children heard his steps on the path and out through the gate.

They ran and threw their arms about Nan. "Oh, you saved us!" they cried.

But Nan laughed at that. "He wouldn't have done you any harm. Nothing to be afraid of!"

"Well, perhaps he wouldn't hurt us," Kay said thoughtfully. "But it was rather frightening, all the same. And think how Mother would feel if they said we were the Masker! She wants the village people to like us and be friendly with us. She says we may live here all our lives and that everything depends on their friendliness. She is so sad now because they laugh at us and tease us, and because we hate to go to school. Why, we don't tell her what they do to us any more because it makes her face so sad. And now if they should think one of us was the Masker—well, that would be much, much worse."

"It seemed a nice village, as I came through," Nan said thoughtfully. "It is not right that you should be lonely here. There are plenty of other children."

"Yes," Kay explained. "But we are so slow at learning their language, you see. And we wear such queer clothes, they think. And we are stupid in school. That is dreadful! At home we were never stupid!"

"But you understand all I say quickly enough," Nan wondered. "And you answer without difficulty."

"Yes, but you talk so smoothly, so clearly. Why, I never think about *words* at all when you speak, just about what you mean!" Kay said happily.

"Nor do I," agreed Gentian. "Why, Nan, I believe I would understand what you said in any language. It is odd—and so pleasant!"

"Well, perhaps the village children will forget to wonder at you soon," Nan said, smiling her grave smile. "You can't stay strangers to them always. And now I have a surprise for you—a nice one. Your mother said that I was to take you to buy shoes this morning. She gave me some money for it. Let's clear the table and start right away."

The children were delighted. The shoes they had on were certainly well worn, and Kay's had a hole at the toe. Gentian's were both broken out at the sides. You could see at a glance that they were beyond repair.

"Oh, good!" said Kay. "That will be one thing less for them to poke fun at!"

Very soon they were out on the street, walking toward the stores. They stopped to look in at all the windows. Nan was as interested as they, and did not mind how much they loitered. But at last they reached the shoe store. It was right up against the greengrocer's store with its windows full of vegetables and fruit. In the shoe-store window were shoes of course, several rows of them, smart and shining.

When they got into the store, the first thing they saw

was Rosemarie, the Artist's little granddaughter. She was sitting between her governess, Miss Prine, and her nurse, Polly, being fitted to a pair of white sandals. Her merry brown eyes met Nan's and Gentian's with friendliness. But when they came to Kay's, they said the same thing they always said, as plain as day: "I like you, ever so much. If only we were allowed, we might be such splendid playmates. I have read so many exciting stories that I want to tell you. I like sea stories best, stories of pirates and runaway

boys and hidden treasure. You do too, I know. And I want you to let me climb your tree. You are splendid at climbing. Yesterday I thought you were falling, but you caught yourself. Oh, I do want to play with you!"

"Good morning," Nan said, smiling down into the friendly, merry eyes.

But the governess and the nurse stared coldly and each put a hand on Rosemarie's arm. *Their* eyes said plainly, "What do you mean by speaking to our charge? And who are you anyway? We have never seen you in the village before. But these children you have with you are refugees and you may be, too. We can't be too careful where our special little Rosemarie's concerned. You see that, don't you?"

They said nothing with their voices in spite of all their eyes had said, so Nan could not know their thoughts, for she had turned away to a clerk who had come forward from the back of the store. "Good morning," she now greeted him in her clear, cool voice.

"Good morning," he answered politely enough, but perhaps because his business was shoes, his eyes went at once to their feet. Nan's strange, homemade sandals with their twisted grass straps! He looked amazed. The children's worn, hopeless-looking old shoes. He looked superior.

"What can I do for you?" he asked.

"I want barefoot sandals for this boy and girl, please. Have you some?"

"I think so, but they're expensive, and not very practical for all 'round wear. Some good strong oxfords, now—"

"Oh, but it's summer now—or almost! How expensive are barefoot sandals?"

When he had told her, she shook her head. "No, we haven't enough for that. I am sorry."

"I am sorry too," said the clerk; and just at that point the clerk who was waiting on Rosemarie came to ask his help. He hurried away with her.

"Oh dear! And there isn't another shoe store in town," whispered Kay. He was very crestfallen, and Gentian's blue eyes were misty.

"Let us make certain of that before giving up," Nan answered, reassuringly. "I thought I saw another shoe store right beside this as we came in. We can try there."

"Oh no. That was the greengrocer's. Didn't you see all the vegetables and fruit in the window? And the other side is the stationer's."

But Nan shook her head. "I saw a barefoot sandal in the window. I only came on here, past it, because you pulled me."

The children followed her out into the street, hopeful in spite of themselves.

Rosemarie, back in the store, gazed wistfully after them;

but her two attendants looked at each other over her head and laughed.

"Who can that girl be?" Miss Prine wondered. "A queer creature! And did you see the sandals?"

"She's probably the general housework girl the foreigner advertised for, the one who was to 'like children,'" Polly answered. "I never thought anybody'd answer at all."

"Well, this one certainly doesn't look like anybody. So you thought right."

Both Polly and Miss Prine herself laughed at this as though it were very clever.

But Rosemarie did not laugh, and she did not understand why they laughed. Perhaps that was because she had only half heard what they said. Her real thoughts had followed away after Kay and Gentian into the spring sunlight.

And Nan too! Nan had been to Rosemarie like a being made out of sunlight in the dim store. Her voice, asking for barefoot sandals, so clear, so cool, had sounded like the stream flowing through her grandfather's tulip garden. Rosemarie's feet wanted to get up and follow Nan out into the sunshine, out into the spring morning.

But her attendants wedged her in from either side, and the clerk was trying on another white sandal. Rosemarie remembered that she was not allowed to play with village children, to say nothing of these strangers! She shut her eyes so that the clerk might not look up and see them. They were merry no longer. They were more misty than Gentian's had been!

Chapter 4

Kay and Gentian are Measured

As for Kay and Gentian, when they got out into the spring sunshine, they were surprised to find that Nan had been right after all. There was a little narrow door squeezed in between the door they had just left and the greengrocer's. And beside the door was a very small window with one barefoot sandal standing alone in the middle of the display case.

"Why, this was never here before!" Kay exclaimed. "I know perfectly well."

"It is such a little window and such a little narrow door you may have overlooked it," Nan said.

But Kay shook his head. He was sure that it had not been there yesterday when he went to school. He had stopped to look at the shoes in the regular shoe store next door, wondering when his mother would be able to buy him and Gentian some new ones. If the tiny window with its one sandal had been there then, he would have noticed quickly enough, and guessed that since it was so small, its prices might be lower.

But now that the children were close to the little window, they saw that it was not like glass at all. It was dimmer than glass, and yet clearer at the same time. The sandal seemed a long way off, as though they were looking at it through very deep but very clear crystal water. And it was not a leather barefoot sandal. It looked alive, somehow, and it was the color of silver, and tremulous with light. They did not remember all this until later though, for Nan had pushed open the door and they followed her in.

They were surprised to find the little shop so light. How could it be, with such a tiny window? But right away they saw that the light came from above, spring sunlight as bright and full as in a garden. The walls of the shop were blue, the color of the sky. Kay felt that he could walk through any one of the four walls right away, for after all they did not seem like blue walls at all—more like blue air. The floor was just clean, white sand.

There was no one in the shop when they entered. But the opening door had started up a little ovenbird. His wings whirred past their faces and he soared up, up—singing his sudden delightful flight song. They had only time to glimpse his olive-green back, his white breast with the dark spots and his orange crown before he was gone.

"He must be the signal that customers have come," Nan said, looking up after the song.

"How strange!" thought the children. "Why, he takes the place of a bell! But how do they ever keep him from flying off, for there isn't a roof away off up there! There is only the sky, surely."

The ovenbird's song must have been a signal though, for at that instant a clerk came through the side of one wall as though through a curtain.

He was an old man, but very tall and thin and straight. And he was dressed in a long blue robe, with a blue hood. It was not air-blue like the curtains, but more night-blue like a spring dusk. From under the hood his eyes, dark and piercing, yet kindly too, looked at the two children, and at Nan. Then, like the clerk in the store next door, he looked down at their feet.

"These children are in search of sandals, I see," he said. "But you," to Nan, with a keen glance at her, "have made some for yourself as fine and serviceable as any I could possibly get for you."

Nan nodded. "Yes, but Kay and Gentian do need some badly. Have you any barefoot sandals to fit them?"

"I have," said the Shoeman. "But of course I must measure the children if I am to be sure I have any that will fit."

The children glanced about for a bench on which to sit so that the Shoeman might measure their feet. But there was no bench there, and nothing at all in the little shop, no shelves, shoe boxes, no counter, no cash register, nothing but the blue curtains and the sunshine—and the little ovenbird who had come back to his oven-shaped nest and his little mate who was sitting on her eggs. The nest was in some grass, growing in the sand at the foot of one of the blue curtains.

Nan seemed surprised by nothing. She acted as though this might be any store, and not just the strangest store in the world. And the Shoeman did not notice the children's wonder but went about measuring them in a matter-of-fact way. But such a way to measure! He went first to Gentian and tilted her face up toward the sunny distance. Then bending down a little from his tall height, he looked several seconds into her blue eyes. His own eyes never wavered in their piercing but quiet gaze. Nor did Gentian's eyes waver, for she almost saw strange things deep in the old man's eyes, things that she had no words to describe afterward. And she looked steadily, trying to see more.

The Shoeman straightened up. "Yes, you do well to bring her here for shoes," he said. "Her measure is A-x and she will want silver!"

"How can he measure our feet by looking into our eyes?" the children puzzled.

Then the Shoeman moved to Kay, and bending, measured his eyes with his piercing, quiet gaze. Kay's look did not wander either; it was sure and straight. But Kay afterwards said that the Shoeman's eyes had been just eyes, and that the vast distances and golden fields that Gentian had *almost* seen there did not show to him at all.

The Shoeman said, "Very good also! Very good indeed! He will want gold. A-n."

Then he went away up some narrow stairs at the farthest end of the shop. The children had never seen such high, steep stairs before, and they ended just in clear light. When the Shoeman had climbed up and up and reached the light, he went behind it as behind a curtain. A clearer, more crystal light than sunlight shone out a second as he moved through.

The children stood looking up and wondering all the minutes that he was away, until the crystal light shone out again, and the Shoeman came down the stairs with a pair of sandals in each hand. They were such beautiful sandals, the children could only stare.

They sat down on the floor to put them on. The Shoeman had been right in his measurements; they fitted exactly. But Gentian, in spite of her shining eyes and her great delight in the beautiful sandals, looked doubtful.

"You see, for us they ought to be *durable,*" she said. "We have to wear them for such a very long time. These are so light and so delicate—I am afraid Mother would be troubled!"

But she said it very wistfully indeed, for never had she even dreamed that such light, beautiful footwear could be in the world.

But the Shoeman reassured her. "These are durable," he said. "Made indeed of the most durable thing in the world. You may outgrow them, but you can never wear them out."

At that, Gentian was relieved and glad. She looked at the sandals more closely, and saw that they were covered with little silver bees, butterflies, birds, flowers, and even little silver rivers running down to little silver seas. She was overjoyed.

Just as Kay was putting his golden sandals on, the oven-bird suddenly whirred up again, singing his bubbling, sudden song, for the street door had opened and another customer come in. Gentian heard Kay gasp, and turned her eyes away from her lovely new sandals to see why. Then she too gasped, and stared wide-eyed. For there stood the Wind Boy!

No, of course it was not the statuette their mother was making, come to life. Such things don't happen. It was the real Wind Boy, the model for Mother's statuette. The Boy himself. Big. No one could doubt it. And so much more alive!

The thick clustering curls on his head were the color of the morning rays of the sun, and as gleaming. He was taller than Kay by two heads, and slim but sturdy. He was dressed in a purple tunic that did not come to his knees. And his face and arms and neck and legs were touched with the sun to golden brown. His tall purple wings were folded down his back, and so the children just at first did not see them. Kay's father in the happy past years had told Kay many of the old Greek myths, and now Kay thought, "The Wind Boy is one of the gods." But Gentian thought, "He is the nicest boy I ever saw, except Kay, and he is so different from Kay that he mightn't be a boy at all!"

"Well," said the Shoeman, turning to the newcomer, "do you want sandals too?"

The Wind Boy nodded and came nearer. The children

saw now that there was a cloud in his eyes, and across his bright brows. He did not look as though he remembered his wings, or that he could fly.

"I shall have to measure you, you know," said the Shoeman.

The children were surprised to hear that the Shoeman's voice was rather stern.

Then he tipped the Wind Boy's face up to the sunny distance and bent above his eyes. The Wind Boy's eyes did not waver, but Gentian, sitting on the sand near his feet, saw him clench his hands as though he were trying hard at something.

The Shoeman looked longer into the Wind Boy's eyes than he had looked into Kay's and Gentian's. But at last he turned away with a deep sigh. "Have you found the mask yet, and destroyed it?" he asked.

"No, no," cried the Wind Boy, "but I have hunted and hunted, and tried so hard!"

"I am sorry," said the Shoeman, not looking any more at the Wind Boy, "but you don't measure for any of my sandals."

At that, a strange and surprising thing happened. The Wind Boy suddenly threw himself down beside Gentian where she sat on the sand, and looking straight at her began speaking very fast.

"Oh, I did make the horrid mask," he said. "I did wear it and frighten the children. I thought it would be such fun. I made it out of leaves and stems and bark and grass. I worked hard, and thought it was very clever. Then I went out with it, laughing behind it all the time. But when the children ran and screamed with such terror, and one little fellow tumbled down and cried bitterly—why, then it wasn't fun any more. I was disgusted with the old mask that had made the little fellow cry. So I threw it away over your Artist's hedge, and wanted never to see it again.

"But someone picked it up. And ever since, whoever it was that picked it up has been wearing it at twilight to frighten the children. You are a human child yourself, even if you are here in the Clear Village with a pair of the Shoeman's best sandals on. Can't you help me? Can't you tell me who picked up that mask and is wearing it? For until I get it back and destroy it so that it can never frighten any child again, none of my own playmates can play with me, or be anything but kind and sorry, like the Shoeman here. Can't you help me?"

Gentian was all eagerness and pity.

"No, we don't know either who has the mask and wears it at twilight," she said as quickly as the Wind Boy had spoken, and looking straight at him. "But I will help you, Wind Boy, if I can. And Kay will help too, I know. Together we ought to get it back. Then you will tear it all to pieces and be happy again.—But I don't see why you need be unhappy anyway, since it isn't your fault any more. It's not you who are wearing it at twilight," she added.

"Some day you will understand about that, you and the Wind Boy too," said the Shoeman.

But Gentian and the Wind Boy hardly heard the Shoeman's words. They were looking at each other with great friendliness. Gentian whispered comfortingly, "Don't mind. Kay and I will help, truly."

By now Kay's sandals were buckled. They fitted and were very nearly as beautiful as Gentian's. The pictures on these sandals were in gold; there were trees and mountains, deer running in gardens, and waterfalls. In Kay's heart he wondered what the boys in the school would say to these. Would they laugh? Well, let them. For once he would not care, for he could trust the Shoeman.

But now Nan was offering the Shoeman the money that Detra had given her for the shoes. The children suddenly held their breath, for after all, it might not be enough. Indeed, how could it be enough for such beautiful sandals!

The Shoeman counted it over on his palm. Then he handed it back.

"The old woman at the door in the sunshine outside will take it," he said, "and give you a receipt. She is my cashier today."

So Nan thanked him, and the children thanked him, and they went out the door. Gentian was the last out, and she turned to look at the Wind Boy over her shoulder. He was gazing after them ever so wistfully, his wings dropped down his back.

"Oh, come," she called. "Come to play with us."

With a glad bound he was at her side, and followed through the door.

The Shoeman looked long after his customers with pleasure in his eyes. "Gentian measured perfectly," he said to himself as though it were a very pleasant thing. "And I think she *will* help the Wind Boy, and then he shall have his sandals too." Then he stepped away through the blue curtains, and only the two little oven birds were left in the shop.

Outside at the door an old woman sat, selling pencils. She looked very poor with her ragged shawl and patched skirts. And she was lame, for a crutch lay by her side. She was seated on a camp stool and the pencils were spread out on a board across her wide lap. The children had seen her many times before on their way to and from school. For every day in sun or rain she came here to sell her pencils.

"This must be the old woman I am to pay," Nan said to the children. And stopping, she handed the old woman the money that Detra had given her for the shoes. The old woman seemed very much surprised at so much money, and all the hundreds of wrinkles in her face turned merry.

"Thank you and thank you," she said, and began counting out pencils. "Why, it just takes every last one!"

"All the better," answered Nan. "Now you can go home

and spend the day with your grandchildren. It is Saturday and they will be home from school. Perhaps you will tell them stories."

"You are right," said the old woman. "They like my stories, I can tell you, and it's little time I have to give them." She got up and, gathering her shawl around her, hobbled off happily on her crutch.

Gentian and Kay now looked at all the pencils that were theirs with wonder. They never had had enough before, for they were forever drawing pictures. These would last a year at least!

"But I don't see what good it does the Shoeman, or why the pencils are receipts," puzzled Kay.

"Can't you?" said Nan with her gravest smile. "But we can trust the Shoeman and do what he says. There is *some* reason in it somewhere, we may be sure."

Yes, the children could surely trust the Shoeman. They would never forget him and his kind, piercing eyes; and Gentian would never forget the things she had almost seen in those eyes.

Kay walked with Nan. But Gentian was already far ahead with the Wind Boy. They were holding hands and running very fast indeed, Gentian's coppery braids and the Wind Boy's sunlit curls blowing back in the soft spring breeze. Straight down the street they ran and around the corner, already comrades.

Chapter 5

The Keepsake

B UT no one on the street turned to look at them as they ran. That was strange; for surely it is not every day in the week one sees a Wind Boy with fluttering curls and purple wings and bare brown feet racing beside a little human girl on the main street of a village. And now I must tell you why people did not look and stare and point. It was simply because they did not see the Wind Boy at all! How was that?

—Well, have you ever seen a Wind Boy? Still, sometime one must have passed you or met with you in your walks and play. Why it is that we cannot see the Fairies or the Clear People or a Wind Boy, I do not know. But it is true that very few people can, and even those who have the sight for these Other People have not *always* the sight. Sometimes it forsakes them for days together.

But Gentian could see the Wind Boy clearly enough, and Nan could, and Kay. For a minute I thought that the new sandals might have had something to do with that. But on second thought, I am sure not. For they would never have got the sandals at all unless they had had the sight.

Gentian already knew that there was something strange about her sandals besides their strange beauty. Never had she been able to run half so fast before, and never had her body been so light. She scarcely felt her feet on the pavement at all in her running, and she got the idea that there were wings on her feet that would carry her away into the spring air, if she only knew how to use them. But that may have been only because the Wind Boy had her by the hand.

But with Kay it must surely have been his sandals; for before Gentian and the Wind Boy had reached the little swinging gate of home, he had overtaken them. And strange to say, Nan in her homemade grass sandals was ahead of them all!

They met, laughing, at the gate.

"I am going to wash the sitting-room windows and start luncheon now," Nan said as calmly and sensibly as though she had not just been running faster than the wind and got all the spring sunshine somehow into her eyes and hair. "You children had better run away and play. The Artist's gardens are a fine place for that," she added, standing on tiptoe on the doorstep to look over the lilac hedge.

"Oh, Mother doesn't let us go there," Kay cried. "She thinks the Artist wouldn't like it."

"There are no no-trespassing signs," wondered Nan.

"No, but still nobody does go into those gardens—none of the village children."

"But see," Gentian spoke softly, but with great excitement, pointing. "See the gardens and the house just *over* the Artist's house! Why, how, how——?"

Then Kay and Nan saw. A little higher than the Artist's house rose the pillars and arches and vine-wreathed windows of a nobler house; and about it and stretching away at the back of it were gardens and gardens, golden and blue with spring flowers, and long stretches of green grass, and beyond that the forest, and towering above the forest, away, away, the mountains!

How can I tell you, so that you will see a little of what they saw? It was not the Artist's house, nor his gardens, nor was it the wood that you could see any day, nor the same purple mountains beyond. The children knew the sight of all these very well. It was a dimmer but clearer scene, raised a little in the blue spring air. It was dimmer because they were looking at it as though through a crystal, but it gave promise of being clearer if one could only get through into the crystal.

"That is my land," the Wind Boy said while the cloud grew a little darker over his bright brows and darkened his clear eyes. "But I cannot be at home there any more until I have found that mask. No one can play with me. I wander alone; and wherever I come the Clear Children leave."

"Your land is like ours. Only it is as though we were looking at it up through a clear crystal spring," Gentian wondered. "As though through the spring we found in the woods last Sunday."

But Nan who seemed never to be surprised by anything said, "Yes, the Clear Land does seem very like this land at first glance, Gentian. But then when you know it a little better you find it is not like this at all, so very, very different. But then comes the strange part; when you know it even better than well, when you are perfectly at home there, then you see again that it is very like this lower land!"

The children looked at Nan, puzzled. How could she know about all this, and be so sure, when she had only just come from the mountains?

The Wind Boy looked at her, puzzled too, but only by her words.

"Why, you don't believe that no matter how well you came to know the Clear Land, you'd ever think that shoe store where I first found you was like the shoe store next door to it, would you?"

Nan nodded. "Yes, I do."

Gentian clapped her hands. "Oh, was the shoe store where we got our sandals in your Clear Land? That Land?" She pointed.

"Yes, of course," the Wind Boy said, surprised. "Didn't you know that the Shoeman who measured you was one of the Clear People, one of the Clearest?"

"But look!" Kay cried now, pointing above the roof of their own little brown house. There, deep through the crystal was another little brown house. "Oh, there are two of everything, stores, houses, gardens, mountains! Look! Look!" And he pointed down the street to where, above other houses and other gardens, higher houses and higher gardens showed in the crystal. Over the whole village another village hung, overlapping it in places, sometimes hardly to be kept apart from it.

The children gazed and gazed.

"Come," cried the Wind Boy then. "Come with me up into it!"

But how were they ever to get into it! There it was, that other village, clear as light to their eyes, but so distant from their understanding that they did not see how they were ever to get into it. For no matter how near another world may be, it is not so simple to step into it as it is to step into another room. The children knew that without being told. Perhaps it was the crystal light about the Clear Land that they felt they could not get through.

But the Wind Boy laughed at their doubt. He took Gentian's hand and she took Kay's, and they started running.

Nan waved them good-by and went in to her window-washing.

They ran around behind the little brown house, jumped the low rope fence there and were away over the fields at the back. As they ran, Gentian and Kay felt lighter and lighter, until soon they knew that they were running just a little above the ground on a path of blue spring air. Higher and higher their sandaled feet trod the blue air—until they had broken through the crystal light and were in the Clear Land. They stopped by a lilac hedge, laughing with delight.

"Our Great Artist lives in there," the Wind Boy said, pointing proudly.

"Oh, how can he?" cried Gentian. "Aren't we up in the Clear Land?"

"Yes, of course, I don't mean your Artist down there. I mean our Artist up here. Not the one who doesn't want children in his gardens!"

At that minute they heard happy laughter and running feet beyond the lilac hedge. Down the grassy walks of the Great Artist's garden boys and girls came running. They were all in fluttering blue and yellow, purple and silver tunics, and most of them in sandals like Kay's and Gentian's. They were the Clear Children.

Seen fleetingly as they ran on and past, they seemed to Kay and Gentian strangely like their own schoolmates. But when some of them came to the hedge and stood looking over with wide, clear eyes, they looked unlike any human children Kay and Gentian had ever seen. There was a light across their brows and over their smiles that human children never have.

"Oh, have you come to play with us?" asked a little girl in blue. And all the Clear Children looked at Gentian and Kay with curious eyes. "Did you bring them, Wind Boy? And, oh, have you found the mask? We were watching the Great Artist painting up in his studio, and we saw you coming from the studio windows. We thought you must have found the mask!"

But the Wind Boy did not answer, and Kay and Gentian were too shy. You see, their schoolmates down in their village had laughed at them and teased them and not wanted their friendship. So here, even in this Clear Land, they were a little doubtful of friendliness.

The Wind Boy was standing, head dropped, digging his bare toes into the soft turf.

"Say you've found the mask and torn it up," cried a boy about his own height, jumping the hedge and going up to the Wind Boy.

The Wind Boy shook his head without looking. "Not yet," he said.

All the Clear Children fell silent at that and grew troubled for a minute. Then, as though they had forgotten the

Wind Boy, they turned back to one another and their play.
The boy who had gone up to the Wind Boy drew back too,
but before he leapt over into the garden, he smiled at Kay
and Gentian. "Coming?" he asked. "We're off to play hide-
and-seek among the beeches."

"Go on," whispered the Wind Boy, giving Gentian a
shove toward the hedge. "You'll have great fun. I'll stay
around and watch."

"But won't you play too?" asked Gentian, disappointed.

"No. Can't you see they don't want me?"

"If they don't want you I don't want them!" But she
looked wistfully after the Clear Children for all that.

The little girl in blue and the boy who had gone up to
the Wind Boy had not run on with the other children.
They both stayed, waiting.

"Do go!" the Wind Boy urged Gentian and Kay again.
Then he added indifferently and proudly, stretching his
arms, "I'm too sleepy to play anyway."

So Kay and Gentian, with many backward glances toward the Wind Boy, ran away with the Clear Children to
the beech wood.

Never had Kay and Gentian had such fun at hide-and-
seek with playmates, even in their mother country, in their
old home village! One reason, perhaps, was that they had
never before been able to climb the air to hiding places in
trees. If you yourself have never run up and down blue air
with your body as light as a bird's wing, then you cannot
know, you can only dream, what delight was theirs.

At last, at one moment in the game, Gentian ran up the air to the very top of the tallest, biggest beech that she could see anywhere. But she found that a little girl was ahead of her, curled into a nest of forking branches, quite hidden by thick leaves.

Gentian was about to look around for another, lower place to hide, but the little girl whispered her to stay. "There is room enough," she said, curling herself into smaller space against one side of the nest. "See!"

So Gentian crept in beside her and nestled down. "We're like two birds!" she whispered. "Such fun!"

The little girl could not answer at that minute, for they heard the Clear Child who was "it" come running through the woods to stop directly under their tree. But she looked at Gentian, curious but smiling. Then the boy, hunting below, suddenly ran up the air—for his sandals were the kind that let him—and came very near to the girls' hiding place. The two little girls hardly breathed, but their eyes laughed. After a minute the seeker ran on and away, and then they laughed out loud, but softly.

"How could he help seeing us," wondered the little girl in blue—for it was she.

"We were so still," Gentian said. "And the leaves are so thick. I didn't see you, you know, when I came up."

"I am going to tell you my name," the little girl in blue then said softly, and a little shyly. "It is Aziel. Will you call me by it? And will you play with us often?"

"Oh, I will," Gentian promised. How different Aziel was

from the girls in Gentian's school down in the unfriendly village!

"I am Gentian. My father named me that. I live in the little brown house down in the other village—the one beside the Artist's big one. We have only Mother now, for Father went to the war, and we were driven out of our village, and now he cannot find us. Mother says he is hunting and hunting all over the world, and some day he will come to where we are. If he could only know how Kay and I can climb the air now, he would be so glad. He used to make up stories about just such things for us. He had the bluest eyes!"

It was a very long time, indeed, since Gentian had said so much to any stranger. Even when at home, she was apt to think most of her thoughts quietly to herself. But then she had never been with a little girl just her own age who seemed so friendly and understanding.

"What pretty sandals you have," Aziel said. "How splendid that you measured for silver ones!"

"Yours are pretty too! They are so shining!"

"Yes, they have as much light in them as yours. But they haven't all the pictures. And they can't climb the air!"

It was true. Aziel's sandals were shining and beautifully made. But they were blue, and there were only a few bees and birds pictured in them. And they could not climb the air.

"I got mine from the Shoeman in the little store next to the big store down in our village. If you should go there he might give you some just like these."

Aziel laughed merrily. "No, he wouldn't, for he couldn't!" she cried. "Don't you know that he gives you only the sandals that you measure for? Someday, when he tips my face up to the sunlight, I shall measure for silver ones too. Then he will be as pleased as I shall be. He *wants* us all to have silver ones, you know. But I'm better off than the poor Wind Boy. He hasn't any at all!"

Then she added, "If he'd only find the mask and tear it up so that it would never frighten children any more, the Shoeman would give the Wind Boy sandals fast enough, though. He always had silver ones, like yours, Gentian, before."

"But he climbs the air!"

"Oh, that is because he has wings! Of course he can fly. He was born with wings. No matter what he did he would not lose *them*."

But now that Gentian had been reminded of the Wind Boy she was not so happy—not quite. She remembered his proud but shamed look when he said he was sleepy anyway and did not want to play with the Clear Children. Kay had believed him. But Gentian should have known better. She did know better now, remembering his look when he had said it. She knew now that he had not been happy when they had all run off so and left him. Why, he must have felt something the way she and Kay felt when their schoolmates ran away from them, and would not play!

"I'm going to stop playing hide-and-seek and go to find

him," she said suddenly. "It must be horrid not to have anyone to play with! Kay and I always had each other anyway, and he hasn't anybody!"

"But how will you be able to play with him in your silver sandals?" Aziel asked, wondering.

Gentian looked at her, not understanding at all.

"Why, how could *they* keep me from playing with him? I'd rather not have them at all, if they could!"

Aziel stayed very quiet, her eyes dropped, thinking. Then she lifted them and looked at Gentian who was waiting for her to say good-by. "Perhaps you're different. Perhaps you can be like that, because you are a human child, and not exactly like us," she said, but still wonderingly.

But before Gentian said good-by, she reached down into her pocket and took out something. "I want to give this to you, Aziel," she said. "It will be a keepsake, you know." She offered it shyly.

Aziel understood about keepsakes. The Clear Children are not so different from human children as all that. She took it eagerly. It was Gentian's greatest treasure, a piece of quartz, with a bit of gold at its heart.

Aziel was as delighted with it as Gentian had been ever since the hour she found it. "There's a tiny gold bird in it!" she cried, looking closely. "See its wings spread out!"

Gentian caught her breath. "Oh, you see it too? I saw that the minute I picked it up by the spring! But Kay said it didn't look like a bird at all. And even Mother couldn't see it! You will keep it," she added, shy again, "to remember me by?"

"Oh, yes," Aziel promised, her face sparkling, holding it out on her palm in the crystal light.

"Good-by then. I'll come back to play with you some-time soon again." Gentian crept out through the green leaves that closed behind her, hiding Aziel. Then she stood up, and ran down the air to the fern-grown floor of the wood, and sped away to look for the Wind Boy.

Chapter 6

Noon in the Tulip Garden

B<small>UT</small> the Wind Boy was not by the hedge where they had left him. Gentian ran almost the whole length of it calling, "Wind Boy, I've come back to play with you." But no Wind Boy answered.

At last she grew a little discouraged, and in her discouragement she sank back out of the Clear Land. But she sank into the Artist's tulip garden, and that is one of the most beautiful places in the world; so she could not mind too much having lost the Clear Land.

The tulip garden was the very furthest garden in the Artist's estate. Beyond it there were nothing but fields and meadows stretching away to the woods. But it was the most beautiful garden of all, and the most famous. People traveled long distances to see it, and forever after talked of it when tulips were mentioned.

The garden was all in bloom now. There were banks and banks and fields of tulips, red, yellow, white, purple—and all still and brilliant in the noon sun. Right in the center several grassy paths met, and there was a grassy mound that someday was to have a fountain, when the Artist could find a statue beautiful enough and fitting to stand in that place. But Gentian knew nothing of this. She wondered why the grassy mound was there, and why all the paths led to it.

As she drew near to the grassy place she saw right in the center of it a patch of purple. Just at first she thought it was a plot of purple tulips set off by themselves, but she knew better at once; for it was the Wind Boy, lying on his back, with his arms over his eyes, his purple wings wide beneath him. There in the hot noon sunshine, among the still, bright tulips, he was sound asleep.

Gentian crept near on tiptoe. Her approach made not a stir among the flowers, hardly a stir in the air. She went down softly on her knees beside the Wind Boy, for she did not mean to wake him. But for all her care, he stirred in his

sleep. She sank back on her heels, and waited. He flung his arms wide, turned on his side, and then lay still again. The warm noon sunshine was now square in his face, but he did not open his eyes.

"I will stay here quietly," Gentian thought. "I will be as quiet as the sunshine and the tulips. And when he wakes he will be surprised, and glad that I came to find him."

So she waited, looking at him. His wings were purple, the purple of early morning when it touches the tips of tall trees. Gentian knew that purple, for every morning she watched it spread from tip to tip of the cherry-tree boughs outside her window, as the sun was coming up. For one instant all the cherry tree would stand a-gleam with purple aureoled with gold; then it was gone, not to come again until tomorrow as the sun rose. That moment of purple in the cherry tree made Gentian happier than all the cherry blossoms. But she never saw it more than in a flash—not all the tree purple together! And now, here was the same wonderful thing in her new comrade's wings! And she could gaze and gaze, and it never faded!

But for all the purple of his wings, and the sunlight in his curls, Gentian still saw the cloud across his bright brow, and even over his closed eyes, with their golden eyelashes shut down on his cheeks.

"Oh, if I can only help him to find the Masker," she thought, "and get back the mask! I won't be afraid of it any more, anyway. I shall grab at it, as Nan did, or run after it. I'll be braver than the Policeman and cleverer. Oh, I hope it comes tonight, right up to our window again."

But at that minute, she heard steps. The tulips did not stir, but Gentian felt that they began to wait expectantly, and were looking off over one another's heads to see who was coming. They were not heavy footsteps, but that noon stillness had been so very still that sounds could be heard a long way off.

Gentian was troubled, and her heart began to beat very fast indeed. For well she knew that whoever it was would not expect to find a little girl here in the tulip garden, a little village girl who was not allowed here at all. She waited, wide-eyed, troubled.

And then the Artist himself came up a flight of stone steps, and down one of the grassy paths of the tulip garden, toward the place where she waited, kneeling. Gentian had never seen the great Artist so near before, and in spite of her fast-beating heart she looked at him with interest. He was very tall and looked at Gentian's eager eyes like the great Artist that he really was. And Gentian thought strangely, "He is something like the Wind Boy."

Yes, in spite of his being almost an old man, with iron gray hair and many lines around his mouth and eyes, Gentian could see that he was something like the Wind Boy. His hair grew all in thick, clustering curls. That may have been the reason. But I do not think so. I think that Gentian saw deeper than that, and that it was something winged that she noticed.

But whatever it was, it was enough to stop her from being afraid. "He's not so different from the Clear People," she said to herself as he came nearer and nearer down the narrow grassy path.

The Artist was surprised enough to find a strange little girl sitting back on her heels in the very center of his precious tulip garden by the fountain that was to be. But he did not glance about, even for an instant, to see whether any tulips were broken or gone or trodden down, for he knew right at once that this especial little girl had walked softly and loved the garden.

He came quite close to her and stood looking down, not smiling but kindly.

"Good morning," he said. "I didn't expect to find a little girl here, a little stranger-girl that I have never seen anywhere in the world before. Who are you, please?"

But now that Gentian was not afraid of the Artist any more, she remembered the Wind Boy at her knees.

"Sh," she said, her finger to her lips. "Please! He is asleep, you see."

The Artist was puzzled, for he could not see the Wind Boy at all. Perhaps you could not have either, had you been there!

"Who is asleep?" he asked, looking all about.

"Here. The Wind Boy," Gentian whispered. "I found him sound asleep like this. I've been staying still ever since thinking about his purple wings. They are like the morning-purple—only they stay so. The morning-purple goes so quickly you wonder whether it was true. But these you *know* are true."

The Artist still looked down at the little girl, smiling now. He liked her there in her sky-blue frock with her hair the color of shining copper, her blue-gentian eyes looking so friendly up into his. "I must paint her some day like that," he thought. "No child in the village has such fairy-gold hair. Who can she be?"

"So it's the wind that is asleep?" he asked, but softly as she had begged him to. "Yes, I knew that the wind went to sleep some minutes ago, just before the bells rang for noon. But did he go to sleep right here in my tulip garden? And you can see him?"

"No, not the wind itself," said Gentian. "This is the Wind Boy. It isn't quite the same, I think."

Now, because there was something winged about the Artist, he knew that the child might be right, and that the fact that *he* couldn't see had nothing to do with it. So he said, "I will be very quiet then. And you shall go on watching and thinking about the Wind Boy's purple wings. Only do tell me, please, what is your name and where do you live? Or are you a little Wind Girl, who lives in the blue sky?"

Gentian laughed at that, merrily, softly. But she became grave at once.

"I am Gentian," she said. "And I live with my mother and my brother and Nan, who has come to work for us, in the little brown house right by your hedge."

"Really? Then I know who you are. Refugees."

"Yes, foreigners."

The Artist looked down sharply at the way Gentian said

that. "The little girl has been made to feel strange here in our village," he thought, and did not like it.

For although the Artist was so great and famous, and what is called a citizen of the world, still he had now made this village his home, and loved it. Sometimes he felt like a father to it, indeed, for many of its good things, its library, its beautiful school building, its concerts he had given it. He did not like to think that these refugees here at his very gate had been treated unkindly. He did not see how anybody *could* treat this little copper-haired girl unkindly.

"I have a little granddaughter, Rosemarie. Do you ever play with her?" he asked. "*She* doesn't call you 'foreigner,' does she?"

Gentian shook her head. "No, we can't play with her, ever, so she doesn't call us anything. Her governess doesn't let her play with village children. This morning, in the shoe store, she pinched her arm—not to hurt but to remind her."

The Artist looked very grave. He stood for a whole minute in silence. "So she isn't allowed to play with you?" he said at last. "I must ask Miss Prine why. I am not at home all the time, you see, Gentian, and I am afraid I don't know very much what Rosemarie is or isn't allowed to do. Tell me, whom does she play with?"

"No one. She's always alone. We watch her sometimes, over the hedge. Her governess or the nurse is always near. But Rosemarie smiles at us, and *almost* speaks. We like her."

"I am glad you like her. But when you come into the gardens as now, doesn't she play with you then?"

"Oh, but we never play in here. Mother wouldn't let us. We play in our own garden, or in the fields behind our house."

"But you are here now! How is this?"

Gentian dropped her head. "Yes, but I came down out of the Clear Land—out of the air, you know! I couldn't tell I was landing here. Then I saw the Wind Boy asleep, and forgot I mustn't stay."

"I am glad you did forget, Gentian. But now you have given yourself away! Didn't I say you were a Wind Girl! I knew you came out of the blue."

Gentian laughed her merry laugh. "No, I am a human, truly," she said. "But how can I explain to you?"

"Don't try. Perhaps I can understand without understanding. I am going away now, softly, so as not to wake your Wind Boy. And I must find out why you are not Rosemarie's playmate. But I can't do that today, for I am going away on the train, if you have not made me lose it. I came for a parting look at my tulip garden and to think about the fountain that is to be. But good-by, and when I come again, then I shall see you. If you have not vanished into the blue!"

The Artist went away then as quietly as Gentian could have wished. When he reached the stone steps he looked at his watch, and hurried down out of sight. But all the way to the station, and many many times before he saw her again, he thought smilingly of Gentian, and her talk of morning-purple.

But their voices must have disturbed the Wind Boy after all, for he was stirring again. Gentian stayed still as still—still as the noon sunshine and the tulips; but it did no good. His eyes slowly opened.

Then Gentian, to her great satisfaction, saw that those opening, purple eyes were as clear as Aziel's had been, and as happy. But when they were wide open, they clouded again, as though waking had made him remember the mask and all his troubles.

"Oh, please," Gentian cried, "can't you keep it?" She meant, of course, the clear tranquility that sleep had given.

The Wind Boy at her words sat up quickly, surprised and glad to find her there.

"Where did you come from?" he asked, with his most radiant smile.

"From the beech wood, up in the Clear Land. I came hunting you. I wanted to play with you."

"Really?"

"But now it's noon. The village bells have rung. So I can't stay and play after all, but must run home to dinner. Nan would be sorry if we were late her very first day, perhaps."

"And I must go back to the Clear Land too," said the Wind Boy. "It is time for my work."

"Your work? Do you work?"

He laughed. "Of course. And I can go on with that even if they won't play with me," he added, proudly.

"What do you do?"

"Well, today I'm going to work at pulling weeds with the Great Artist in *his* tulip garden, just up there above this one."

"Does your Great Artist work in his own garden?" Gentian asked, amazed. For why the owner of that tall house that she had seen in the Clear Land, the house with its arches lost in the sky, should come down out of it to pull weeds in his own garden, she did not see.

But the Wind Boy was laughing at her surprise, though friendlily. "Of course he does. Why not?"

Gentian could not say why not. "Does Aziel work?" she asked instead.

"Why, of course. Did you think she only played?"

"Yes."

"Don't you work?"

"Of course I do. I help Mother and I even mend sometimes—though I'm not very good at that yet! I help Kay weed the garden, too, and much more. But I'm not a Clear Child."

At that the Wind Boy did a surprising thing. He said, "I think you're nicer than a Clear Child. I like you best," and he bent and kissed her on the mouth.

Then he laughed and backed away over the grass and down among the tulips. He was a little embarrassed, but he was not ashamed. Gentian stood where he had left her, wide-eyed, surprised.

"Good-by," he called and turned and ran right away over the tulips. He ran very fast, and soon began to climb the air, his purple wings spread wide. Almost at once he was lost to Gentian's sight in the dazzling noon sunlight.

Gentian was so taken by surprise and by happiness, too, that she stood still looking up into the sunlight for some time after he had gone. Unless a Wind Boy has kissed you at noon in a tulip garden, you cannot know why Gentian stayed so still, wide-eyed and thoughtful. All in a flash she had learned about comradeship, the comradeship that may be between a human child and a Clear Child.

But after a while she remembered the tulips. Why, he had backed right down into them, and then turned and run through them! They must be trampled and crushed!

She ran to look. But not one single tulip was even bent. They were all straight and lovely. But they were swaying slightly in a breeze that Gentian could scarcely feel. She spoke to them gravely. "Oh, he ran over you," she said. "That is why you are so smiling and blowing! But he kissed me."

Then she ran away down the grassy path to the stone steps, down those, across a wide lawn yellow with jonquils, and away to the hedge, which she crawled through. She remembered, as she ran, that it was Saturday and Mother would be at home for dinner and the rest of the afternoon.

Kay was there ahead of her, for he had remembered about Mother too. He had heard the village bells ringing for noon, even while he played in the air with the Clear Children, and he had found the way back as quickly as he could. Mother was sitting on the step and Kay was beside her, still a little breathless from his hurry.

"Such a day!" he was saying. "And thank you, Mother, for those beautiful sandals."

"Oh, see mine too," Gentian cried, as she threw herself down on the step at her mother's knee.

"Yes, they are very nice sandals. And they look strong enough to last all summer," Detra said. "Nan did very well."

But the children hardly heard her words, for they were staring in sad amazement at their feet. Where were Gentian's silver, pictured sandals, and where were Kay's golden ones? These things on their feet were just strong, sensible leather—the kind of sandals all the children in the village were wearing this spring!

Where? How?

Nan had just come to the door to say that dinner was ready, and she saw the children's sorry faces.

"Oh, don't be troubled," she comforted. "They are the very same sandals we got, truly. Only you see in the store you were looking at them in the Clear Light. Now it is the Earth Light. When you go back into the Clear Light, you will find they are not changed a bit. Yours will be silver there, Gentian—and yours gold, Kay."

The children were glad and relieved. But Detra did not understand what it was all about. She thought it must be some game the three had been playing together, however, and did not ask questions.

"Were they magic sandals?" you ask.

Not a bit of it. For one thing, I do not believe in magic, and so you will not find any in my story. It was really very simple. Think about it for yourself. Why need a thing in Clear Light look at all the same as it looks in the denser light of the sun? It would be more like magic if it did, I should say.

The children, of course, were full of their adventures in the Clear Land.

"Oh, you ought to have stayed, Gentian," Kay cried, when they had washed their hands and had come to the table. "I was 'it' finally. And where do you suppose that little blue girl hid?"

"Aziel, do you mean?" asked Gentian, proud to know her name. "She was in the top of the tallest beech when I left her."

"Oh, yes. She was found there, and didn't get her goal because she couldn't run down the air, but had to climb all the way down through the branches. But when I was 'it' later, I saw her run right into the Artist's house to hide. She was late in finding a place, and I had done all the counting and opened my eyes—and there she was whisking in at the big front door. We were playing around the house then."

"I hope you didn't follow her," Detra said, a little anxiously, for she thought they must be talking about some game of hide-and-seek with the village children.

"But I did. I ran right after her before I had time to think, and found her way up many, many flights of stairs hiding behind the Artist's easel! There was a big picture on it that quite hid her. I beat her to the door, and down the stairs, and would have got her goal but I tripped over a rug at the foot of the very last one. She jumped right over me, laughing and got there first."

But Detra, their mother, was aghast.

"Kay! Kay! How could you!"

Then how Kay and Gentian, too, laughed! "Oh, not that Artist, Mother. I mean the Great Artist, the one who lives in the air!"

Detra sighed relief. She was sure now that the children were just talking about imaginary adventures. So she showed no surprise when Nan, who had come in with some hot biscuits and heard Kay's story, now said, "The Artist they mean is very different from your Artist over the hedge there. No one need be afraid of him. Children are as free to run in and out of his house as the air is free to blow in and out."

Detra smiled up at her, taking a biscuit, not understanding a bit, but glad that Nan was already such friends with the children.

Chapter 7

The Spring in the Woods

SATURDAY afternoons and Sundays were the best part of
the whole week for Kay and Gentian, for their mother
was at home then, and could go on walks with them and
tell them stories. The walks were usually out across the
meadows that lay behind the little brown house toward the
woods and the purple mountains. They never could reach
the mountains in just an afternoon's walk, of course, but
they liked even going toward them. And on those days
when they walked rather fast, and did not ask for too many
stories by the way, they did reach the woods.

Detra made up the stories during the week, while she
worked at her machine in the roaring factory. That was
odd, for these stories were all about the woods and fields
and streams and the people, unseen by mortals, who dwell
in them. Those were the stories she made up. But there
were others about great men of distant times and far-away
countries. And added to these were the myths of their own
land, the land they had perhaps left behind them forever.
The children liked the myths the best.

Between the stories they would talk together about Hazar, the father who had lost them, and was now hunting them over the world. Indeed, Detra talked about him so much and kept him so alive in the children's minds that forever after, when they remembered those Saturday afternoons, it seemed as though their father had been with them on the walks.

Today, though, there were no stories. The children were too full of their adventures in the Clear Land to talk about anything else. And besides, Nan was with them. Detra had helped with the dishes so that she might come. For Detra knew from the very first that Nan would be at home in the fields, walking toward the mountains. She was rather like one of those tranquil people that moved through Detra's dreams while she sat or stood in front of her machine in the roaring factory. She thought it more and more while she listened to Nan's voice answering the children, and saw her short curls blown about in the sun.

But Detra hardly listened to what the three were saying; for it was all talk of the Clear Land, and Detra still had an idea that that must be a game Nan was playing with the children. So she did not interrupt them, but thought her own thoughts instead. They were thoughts of Hazar. Would he ever find them?

And so thinking her own thoughts, Detra gradually fell behind. Her children and Nan were walking as though they meant to reach the mountains. Indeed, half the time they did not walk at all, but ran and danced, as children run and dance in the Clear Land.

At last the three came to the spring in the wood. There it lay, cupped deep in green and silvery moss.

"See," whispered Gentian. "When you look deep down into it, bending close above, it is like the Shoeman's window, only with bright pebbles instead of a silver sandal away off down there."

Nan stretched herself out on the silvery moss and looked down long into the crystal water.

"It is like the window, isn't it?" Kay asked. "And it's like the air around the Clear Land too, once you think of it."

"Yes, it is like both," Nan agreed.

Gentian pulled at Nan's wood-brown frock. "Do you think, Nan, we might get through into the Clear Land by way of this spring?"

Nan sat up. "Yes. I think you might. But it would be harder getting back this way, when once you had gone. If I were you, I would not hurry things, but wait until the Clear Land showed itself to me again without my trying."

Gentian now stretched herself out on the moss and looked down into the clear water as Nan had done, her face quite close. Nan and Kay wandered off, to look and listen for birds. Kay knew rather a lot about birds, and was forever adding to his knowledge. It was a proud time for him now when he could display his lore before Nan—Nan who listened so quietly and was such a splendid companion.

Gentian hardly knew they had gone. She was gazing at the shining, smooth, many-colored pebbles down at the bottom of the water. They were pink and purple, blue, green and white. But besides these fascinating colored ones, there were many uninteresting gray ones. They were uninteresting only at first glance, however, for almost at once Gentian found that it was the gray pebbles she looked at most. She saw now that they were dove-gray and worn so smooth, so smooth! Then the longer she looked, the more surely she saw that the gray was just a mask for other color, not pink and purple, blue, green and white—but all those mingled. The smooth gray pebbles, now to Gentian's eyes, were pieces of rainbow.

Then her gaze drifted to the center of the spring where the crystal water, pure and clear and cold, welled up from under a ledge of gray rock, a rainbow rock. As Gentian looked, her heart beat fast and her lips smiled, for she was learning the secret of the rock. What that secret was I cannot tell you, for Gentian says it is not a secret in words—you must just know it without words, that is all!

Kay and Nan, by this time, had wandered beyond her hearing, and the birds that had flown away when the three had come to the spring now returned. Gentian heard them singing above her. One little yellow-throat, fairy-like behind his black mask that had nothing frightening about it, came and perched on a young birch shoot just at her shoulder. There he sang his "Witchery, witchery, witchery!" over and over. His mate was there too, without any mask. They never minded Gentian for she was lying so still, perhaps they thought she was just part of the wood.

But a strange thing was happening to Gentian now, in

spite of all her stillness. She was looking down through the
crystal spring into the Clear Land.

"But the Clear Land is up, not down," you cry.

Yes, of course. Well, Gentian was looking up through
looking down, that is all. It can be done.

She was seeing into the Clear Land as through a window pane. The window pane was the crystal spring. But she
would never have known it was the Clear Land, and not
just a reflection of the wood where she lay, had it not been
for the crystal light, for she was looking into another beech

wood, and there was a spring there cupped in silvery and green moss. It was the other spring, of course, the spring that overhung this one where she was really lying.

So far, this other place was the same as that place where she lay, save for the crystal light. But there were two people by that other spring, the Wind Boy—and her mother!

Yes, there was Detra in the Clear Land, sitting back on her heels at one side of the spring; and there was the Wind Boy on the opposite side, lying moody and silent, staring into the water. Gentian had never seen her mother like this. Her face was so shining and carefree. But that was not it. There is no way to tell you—but she was rather like a larger Clear Child.

Gentian was still for a while with wonder. But then she cried, "Mother!"

At her cry the yellow-throat, perched on the young birch shoot at her shoulder, dropped his song in the middle and, startled, flew away.

But Detra did not turn her eyes to Gentian. For Gentian was only seeing through into the Clear Land; she was not in it herself, and there was no way for Detra to see or hear her.

No. Instead of turning at Gentian's cry, Detra smilingly spoke across to the Wind Boy. Gentian heard not a word of what she said nor the Wind Boy's reply. But she could see that the Wind Boy brightened up as he answered, and for the moment forgot his moodiness. And in that moment Detra worked quickly with her strong, beautiful fingers on the little image of the Wind Boy that was standing upright in the moss before her. She was trying to catch the changed look in the plastilina.

But Detra had not had the statuette when they all came across the meadows together! Gentian was sure of that. How was it there with her now, then? And how had she found her way through to the Clear Land?

"Mother," Gentian cried again. And at that second cry, the birds that had alighted farther off than the yellow-throat and had not been disturbed by the first cry stopped their songs too, and flew away. Gentian was left alone in the silent wood. And Detra, seen through the crystal water, did not turn her eyes toward the cry—she only went on working at the plastilina with swift, sure fingers and talking to the Wind Boy. Gentian saw her lips moving.

Gentian was frightened now. She reached toward her mother. At the instant of her gesture the spring was a window no longer; it had become just a spring, and Gentian's arms were in the water. The other spring was gone, the Wind Boy and her mother.

She stood up then and looked all about her in the wood. How silent! Not even the sound of wings stirring amid leaves! She called, "Kay, Kay! Nan! Hello! Where are you gone to? Nan!" at the very top of her voice.

"Hoo-oo," from a long way off through the trees. It was Kay's reassuring voice. And then came "Hoo-oo." That was Nan, clearer and higher, like a bird-call.

Gentian fled from the still spring and ran toward the

voices. She met Kay and Nan in a meadow of bracken in a little ravine.

"What is the matter, Gentian?" Nan asked the minute she saw Gentian's face. "What has happened?"

But Gentian could only say, "Where is Mother? I want my mother."

"Why, we left her at the edge of the woods hunting violets. You know that. It is not far away!"

"Oh, do you think she will truly be there in the sunshine just hunting violets? Do you think so, Nan?"

"Yes. Why not?"

But Gentian found no words for the sadness and trouble of her heart. If you had seen *your* mother so near, and called to her, and she could not hear or see you, I think you would have felt the same.

"Oh, let us hurry then and find her. Hurry!"

So the three ran away through the bracken to the edge of the woods. And there, standing and looking about, they at first saw no Detra. Gentian was about to call "Mother!" in a much louder and wilder way than she had called at the spring. But the call stopped at her lips. For there, just in front of them, down in the grass, a large bunch of gathered violets beside her, lay Detra sound asleep in the sunshine.

Kay thought, "How tired and pale she looks! Oh, why can't I go to work in that roaring factory, and let her stay at home?"

Nan thought, "The sun and the meadow were just what she needed."

But Gentian thought nothing at all. She flung herself upon her mother with a dozen kisses.

Detra sat up, surprised out of sleep, drawing the back of her hand across her eyes. Her dark hair came slipping and sliding down around her shoulders as the pins loosened. Kay found them for her, quickly, searching in the long grass. Then, still sitting there in the sunny grass that came almost up to her shoulders, Detra wound up her smooth hair and pinned it high into place. Her eyes were clear with sleep, and her lips smiling.

Gentian thought, "Why she looks almost the way she looked at the spring in the Clear Land. But where is the statuette?"

Detra, glancing up at her little girl, caught the happy light in her eyes. "What is it, Gentian?" she asked.

But Gentian only asked, "Did you have a dream, Mother, while you slept here? Were you, perhaps, dreaming?"

"No." Detra shook her head, quite certain. "No, no dreams at all. Just deep, deep sleep."

And Detra was right; she had had no dreams at all, only the best sort of sleep there is, out there in the sunshine.

Then they went home across the meadows. Only this time Gentian stayed back with her mother and carried the violets loosely in her skirt, not to crush them.

Nan and Kay went on ahead and were home well ahead of them getting supper ready. But Gentian never told her mother how she had seen her through the crystal spring. It was something more to wonder about than speak of.

Chapter 8

Through Music

THAT night Detra brought out the Wind Boy and worked
on his mouth, trying to make it smile as it should, a
Clear Land smile. But she sighed often, for in spite of her
long sleep and rest in the meadow grass that afternoon she
was not succeeding. Gentian heard her mother's sigh.

"Just wait, Mother darling," she said. "When Kay and I
have caught the Masker and got the mask you can get the
Wind Boy right, for then he will be happy. He will be as
happy and clear-eyed and smiling as the other Clear Children. Only wait for that, Mother!"

Detra drew the back of her hand across her eyes. "Perhaps," she said. "But you must try hard to help him toward
happiness, children, for until he is happy and care-free, how
can I make him so?"

But then she shook herself, as though from a dream,
and pushed the statuette away from her, away to the opposite side of the table. Laughing, she stood up, stretching her
arms out sleepily.

"Come, children," she said. "I am half asleep already, and dreaming. I forgot it was only a game—all your talk about the Wind Boy. It's your bed time, and I'm going too. It's that long walk, and all the fresh air."

How pleasant it was to have Mother going up the stairs with them, and to bed at the same time! Oh, they wished that every Saturday they might go so far that this would happen.

But Nan in spite of the walk was neither tired nor sleepy. When the dishes were done and the floor brushed up, and the milk bottles put out at the back door, she blew out the lamp in the kitchen and went out to sit on the doorstep in the spring starlight.

And as she sat there, her head back against the door-post, her eyes half shut, a sudden breath of sweet wind came down to her out of the cherry tree. She lifted her eyes as though the sweet wind had spoken to her. There was a parting in the high flowery branches, and out through it, from his secret place of watching, came the Wind Boy into the evening air. Softly and lightly on halfspread wings he drifted down and stood by Nan on the doorstep. She moved to one side to make room for him.

"I've been up there all evening watching for that old Masker," he told her. "But it never came at all tonight. And now it won't, I suppose, for it's long past twilight. It's no use."

"Don't give up," Nan said softly, so as not to waken the sleepers in the house. "Other twilights are coming,

and in one of them you will surely get back your mask."

The Wind Boy grew silent. Nan did not look at him, and grew silent too, for she knew that more than he had told her was bothering him. She was sorry, but until he should speak, she did not know how to comfort him.

After many minutes he leaned toward her, putting his hand on her knee. He said, turning his head away, "That little girl asleep up in the house there promised to help me."

So that was it. "She will help you, and Kay will help too. They both mean to. But tonight they were sleepy from their long walk, and besides, this is their mother's day. But when next the Masker comes wandering around in the twilight, be sure Kay and Gentian will be ready."

The Wind Boy raised his head up at that and Nan saw that he was cheerful again, that is as cheerful as he could well be while he was shut away from his Clear Land playmates and must go without his silver sandals.

After that they said no more, but stayed silent and still as the starlight in friendly company. It was late in the evening that the Policeman on his final rounds and taking a last look about for the Masker stopped at the little swinging gate to look hard at Detra's doorstep.

"It almost seems as though there's somebody there," he whispered to himself. But when he had leaned over the gate and looked longer, he shook his head. "Just starlight glimmering on the stone," he smiled to himself. "I'm beginning to see people in mere starlight! Well, that's no worse than seeing mountains in a girl's eyes. What's coming over me!"

Puzzling about the odd tricks he was beginning to play on himself, he moved away toward his home and his bed.

Then came Sunday morning. As always on Sunday

Detra took her children to the village church. Now these children were almost as bewildered in church as in school, and more ill at ease. Partly this was because of their clothes. To church they must wear the same faded blue that they wore to school, and all the other children who came to church with their mothers and fathers were dressed in "best" clothes. Gentian and Kay felt that they were well stared at for daring to go to church in their everyday garments.

But their greatest bother was Detra. She was truly beautiful, their mother, but no one in church could know it. For there she was in her dark cape, the cape she wore to the factory every day and that the children hated. It covered her from her head to her heels. But that was just as well, for under it was only the old black smock dress that she wore daily. Detra, it is true, had embroidered a bright bunch of buttercups on both pockets, and that made it gayer. But the dress was too shabby, in spite of the buttercups, to show at church.

And then she had covered her smooth, dark hair, that looked so beautiful wound high on her head, with a dull-colored scarf. "Why," Kay said to himself now, for the hundredth time as they walked along toward church, "it's just as though Mother were a candle, only all snuffed out by these horrid clothes!"

But the children had never told their mother how they felt about church, and if she guessed, she never told them that she guessed.

The village church was white with a white, high steeple. It stood at the top of a little hill over the town. Today, when the children and their mother reached the hill, they saw that it must be later than they had thought, for there was no one on the sidewalk at all, walking up toward the church. They hurried their pace. And when they reached the door they heard the music of the first hymn. It floated out to them through the open windows.

Oh, this would be worse than ever, going in when everyone was before them and the service begun!

But when they had reached their own places, Kay's heart suddenly glowed. For Rosemarie was there. She stood in her grandfather's pew beside Miss Prine. She was all in white today, with soft hemstitched ruffles at her neck and wrists. Her dancing dark curls were lost under a wide white leghorn hat with a wreath of daisies, buttercups and bachelor buttons around the brim.

But she could not smile at Kay, the smile that said so much, for her pew was way down in front, and Kay could only see her back and now and then the side of her cheek.

This was just a little village church, and so there was no pipe organ to comfort the refugees' hearts with its noble, swelling tones. There was just a little "parlor organ," and Miss Todd, their schoolteacher, was playing it today instead of the regular organist.

"Miss Todd looks different somehow, doesn't she?" Gentian whispered to Kay while Detra was finding the place in the hymn book.

Kay stopped looking at Rosemarie's back and saw that it was true; Miss Todd's church expression was very different from her school expression.

"School puts her out, I guess, the way Mother's clothes put her out," Kay whispered back. And Gentian nodded, for she and Kay understood each other very well, even when queer things like that were said that most people wouldn't understand exactly. At school Miss Todd was very brisk and ready. Here in church, playing the little parlor organ, she was neither brisk nor ready. But she was ever so much more alive.

The children noticed it even more later when she played while the collection was being taken up. Miss Todd looked as though she had forgotten the congregation then, and even the choir. She was thinking only about the music and what it meant.

And suddenly, as Kay and Gentian watched her, they began to hear the real music, the high, noble pipe-organ tones the composer had heard when he wrote the score. This new, rich music carried them away, and they did not think to be startled.

It carried them away into church in the Clear Land.

At least they thought it was church. For there were the Clear Children they had played with yesterday sitting in a large half circle. Were they sitting on a crescent-shaped bench? Kay and Gentian could not be sure, for they only glimpsed them for a second. Their colored tunics and gleaming sandals, and the opal-shaded wings of some, made the half circle seem a rainbow arch dropped upon the grass.

Why the children thought this was church was because of the rapt, uplifted faces of the Clear Children, and the music, oh more splendid and holy than any pipe-organ music, that filled the sky.

Gentian looked toward Kay quickly to see whether he was through into the Clear Land with her. But how she knew where to look—that would be hard to say, for he was sitting on the bench at the very opposite end, at the tip of the crescent. All the Clear Children were between them! He was looking toward Gentian, across the crescent too, and their eyes met for an instant. Then they smiled, for they were glad they had both got through together.

But the music! The whole sky was throbbing with this great music. And in the instant that the eyes of the brother and sister met, the music dropped crystal curtains between them. They could not see each other now, or any of the Clear Children. Kay and Gentian, each sat alone, and looked out into—what? I cannot say. Kay thought afterwards it was the ocean stretching away forever, as far as his sight could reach. But Gentian was sure it was the sky—that she was looking out through the sky forever and forever.

But whichever it was, the crystal clearness of the air made it possible for the eyes of the children to see a much greater distance than they ever could down here in this denser air.

And while they looked out into infinity, the organ

rolled. It shook their very hearts. And then it grew still. But when the organ was stilled, the infinite blue that surrounded the children took up the music, not in their ears, but in their hearts.

No matter how long Kay and Gentian live here on this earth they will never forget that instant of church in the Clear Land.

But it could be only an instant because the deacon, passing the plate for the collection down in the village church, called them back. Perhaps the eyes of the congregation, following the deacon in his plate-passing, helped too in calling them back. For all the people who sat behind them or beside them knew it was their turn to put in their pennies, and expected them to do it. So the children came rushing back from the Clear Land, and gave their mite to the collection.

They could hardly, at first, believe that they were back in the village church again. But there was Miss Todd still playing at the little parlor organ, her face alive. And there was Rosemarie down in front with the bright wreath around her leghorn hat. And there was their mother beside Gentian, but with the far-away look in her eyes that the children very well knew meant she was thinking about Hazar, their father. And hadn't they just dropped their pennies into the bronze plate? Oh yes, this was real enough. They had heard the pennies ring a little on the metal. Things in a dream don't ring like that. But even so, it was hard for the children to believe that the village

church was real, so suddenly they had come back into it—
and so shadowy for a while it had seemed.

As they were walking home, one on each side of Detra,
Kay said across to Gentian thoughtfully, "I don't think I
shall ever mind having to go to church in old clothes again.
It doesn't seem to matter any more."

Gentian had been thinking the same thing. She wanted
to tell Kay so and to say that now, all because of that
instant of church in the Clear Land, she was seeing everything that touched her little life in *proportion*. But she had
no words for this, and so she was silent, thinking.

In the afternoon they sat in the shade of the cherry tree,
while Nan read aloud from one of their favorite books, and
Detra rested upstairs on her bed. Toward twilight, the first
thunder shower came up. It began with a low rumble away
off somewhere beyond the purple mountains.

"Oh dear," Kay muttered. "If it rains the Masker won't
be out. I hope it doesn't rain till dark."

"I thought you didn't like the Masker coming around,"
Nan smiled.

"Oh, but you see we're going to catch it, and get the
mask away for the Wind Boy. Everything is different now,"
said Kay.

But their fears were justified. By twilight great sheets of
warm spring rain were driving across the little garden, and
the children were inside, kneeling on the bench, looking
out disappointedly into the growing dark.

"Well, there's tomorrow's twilight," Nan comforted them.

Yes, but before tomorrow's twilight could come they must go to school, for tomorrow was Monday. And the children were in the habit of dreading Mondays as much as they looked forward to Saturdays. They were, you see, already forgetting a little the new sense of proportion they had discovered in church that morning. But though tomorrow was Monday, it was to be quite different from any other Monday. You shall hear about it.

Chapter 9

The Other School

THAT Monday morning, the minute Gentian and Kay
had slipped into their seats, they looked to see if Miss
Todd had kept her Sunday face, the face that was so alive.
But alas, she had not. Now she was her school self again,
brisk and businesslike. But the aliveness was gone.

She began the morning with an arithmetic example, the
same for all. "And those who get the correct answer in five
minutes shall have turns in making up problems for the
class," she promised. "That will be interesting, won't it?"

Now, although Gentian had been hearing the language
of this adopted country for more than a year, she was still
slow at understanding when anyone spoke as briskly as
Miss Todd always did speak in school. I must tell you that
Gentian was a little slower at everything than Kay. It was
not that she did not think as much and as truly. It was that
she did not think so quickly.

And now she knitted her brow over the very wording of
the example that Miss Todd had dictated. How was she

ever to begin figuring until she remembered the meanings of the words? She looked up at the clock with its moving hands. Her cheeks began to get hot. She glanced worriedly across at Kay. But he, all unaware of her trouble, was bent over his paper, his pencil moving surely and swiftly. If he had understood, why couldn't she?

On the way back to her paper her eyes met Miss Todd's inquiring ones.

"What is it, Gentian?" Miss Todd asked. "If you have your answer already, please bring it to me."

Miss Todd must have known there had not been time for Gentian to do the problem, especially with her eyes wandering around the room!

Gentian shook her head.

"I suppose that gesture means that you have not the answer yet," Miss Todd said. "Then please attend to your work as the others are doing."

Gentian looked dutifully down at the paper on her desk. But now she found that even the meanings of the few words she had understood when she took them down had left her. The figures and letters danced crazily all together back and forth and up and down on the yellow scratch paper. Her cheeks were getting hotter and hotter, for she felt that Miss Todd was still watching her.

It seemed hours to Gentian before the given five minutes were up. But Miss Todd's words then filled her with dismay. They were: "Now all put down your pencils please, while Gentian gives us her answer."

Gentian looked at Miss Todd with doubtful surprise. Didn't she know that Gentian had not made one mark on her paper! Hadn't she been watching all the time! Yes, Miss Todd's expression told Gentian that she knew. Well then, why—

Gentian dropped her head now in the shame that Miss Todd thought it well for her to feel. "I haven't got the answer," she said in a low voice.

"I don't understand. Don't whisper, please. Stand up and repeat what you muttered, loudly enough for me and your schoolmates to hear."

Gentian stood up by her desk. "I have not got an answer. I have not done the problem."

"Not done it at all? Not even begun?"

"No, not even begun."

Miss Todd was silent at that, and all the children held their breath.

"How many have done the problem?" she at last asked.

Several pupils raised their hands, and Kay was among them.

"You see," Miss Todd said to Gentian. "Many of the others have finished, while you haven't even begun. I know, of course, that you are slower. But you might at least have *tried*."

Again she was silent. Gentian still stood. She was looking at her sandals, for she had not the heart to look anywhere else. What were they all thinking of her! And Kay—oh, how ashamed of his sister he must be!

Miss Todd, out of her silence, came to a decision. "I must do with you then, Gentian, what I have not had to do with another child for years! It is an old-fashioned punishment, and quite out of keeping with my modern methods. But I can think of no better way to impress you with your lack of co-operation. You must wear a dunce cap, and stand in the corner here behind me for half an hour."

A giggle went round the room. But Miss Todd's swift glance sought the gigglers out, and the school was as silent as before. Then she made the high dunce cap, very quickly and expertly, from an old map that she took from a drawer of her desk. She pinned it into shape with pins from another drawer. Then she beckoned Gentian to her, and when Gentian got there, her eyes still on her sandals, her cheeks a hot poppy-red with shame, Miss Todd fitted the dunce cap down on her bright, fairy-gold head. That done, so snugly there was no chance of its tumbling off, Miss Todd turned Gentian about by the shoulders and gave her a gentle shove toward the corner.

How Gentian found the corner safely I do not know, for her eyes were quite blurred with tears that she was steadfastly winking back.

"Now," Gentian heard Miss Todd say to her other pupils, "you are not to stare at Gentian any more. Kay may stand and give us his answer."

Gentian very well knew that Kay's pleasure in being so chosen was entirely spoiled by his shame and sorrow for his sister. Her shoulders began to shake, and two tears es-

caped her hardest blinking and rolled down her cheeks to
splash on the faded blue of her dress, and add to its dim-
ness.

"Oh, I mustn't, I mustn't cry out loud!" she said to herself. "Kay would never forgive me! I must stop, stop, *stop!*"

Now Gentian, in spite of all her gentleness, was a brave
little girl. And using all the braveness that was hers, she did
manage to wink her tears away. The minute they were gone
and her eyes were clear, she instantly forgot all her trouble
in her utter surprise at what had happened.

She was not looking at the corner of the schoolroom at
all. No, she was standing just inside another school, and
facing it. She knew at once, by the clear crystal light, that
she had got through her own crystal tears, somehow, to a
school in the Clear Land, the school that hung in the air
above her everyday school! Why, of course, the school
must have its *other* school too, just as the shoe store had its
other shoe store, the Artist's mansion its other mansion rising into the clouds, and the village church its other church!
But she had not thought of that before.

This other school was very different from the school she
had just left back there. Its walls and roof were nothing but
delicate green vines and white starflowers growing on trel-
lises. It was just a big arbor with a grassy floor. And the
pupils were sitting about, cross-legged on the ground. The
Teacher, though, sat at the end of a low, green garden bench,
and she was helping a little Clear Child, the youngest in the
school, with a problem. He was on his knees beside her, on

the bench, leaning against her shoulder, watching the figures she was making on the tablet in her hand.

That was why, just at first, Gentian did not guess that she was the Teacher at all; for in her own school no one would think of leaning against Miss Todd in that happy, carefree way!

But the minute the Teacher spoke, Gentian knew that she must be the Teacher; for her voice had such sure, clear authority! She was looking at Gentian, a little surprised, perhaps, to see a human child standing there in her arbor school.

"What is it, little girl?" she asked. "Do you want something here?"

Gentian did not answer quickly. I have told you she was apt to think slowly. But that was not her only reason for forgetting to answer promptly now. This Teacher was so lovely! Her gown was yellow, and fell from her shoulders in soft folds and trailed out on the grass beside her like a long, wide sunbeam! Her soft, golden hair was braided in two thick plaits that lay down her breasts and hung far below her knees. Around her brow was a shining circlet of star-flowers, violets and hepaticas. And that brow, because she was a Clear Person, was shining and wide.

If *you* had suddenly broken out of *your* school into its other school in the air, and found a Teacher there, all made up of light, would you have remembered to answer her first question promptly? I think I would have done just as Gentian did, and gazed, wide-eyed.

But when Gentian did remember, she said, "Oh, excuse me, please. I am sorry I am so slow! I don't want anything."

"You don't want anything!" exclaimed the Teacher. "Are you sure?"

Gentian laughed then, her merriest laugh, that so few people ever heard. "Well, yes, of course, I want lots of things. I want my father to find us—and I want my mother to have a new frock. I want the Wind Boy to get his mask back, too. Oh, I do want many things."

"But don't you want anything that we can give you here in this school?" asked the Teacher. "You must have come for something."

"I want to be not so slow at problems. But perhaps I was born slow, and nobody can help me there!"

At that, the Teacher laughed, and all her pupils laughed, gaily, musically.

"Of course you're not born slow! What a quaint idea! And that is just why you have come to my school, then—to learn to think quickly. What is the problem that is bothering you at this minute?"

Gentian went to her and showed the paper, which she had kept in her hand. "Here it is," she said. "I can't even understand the words."

"It is the very problem we ourselves were doing when you came up! I am helping little Basil here with his because he is so small." Then the Teacher turned to her school. "Which of you would like to help the little human?" she asked.

All the Clear Children were eager to help Gentian, and

they raised their hands to say so. But one little girl, away at the farther side of the arbor, held up a little stone in her hand and smiled at Gentian. It was Aziel. The Teacher saw the special friendly smile, and the keepsake. "I see that you know Aziel," she said, "so she may be the one to help you."

Aziel rose quickly and came across to where Gentian was standing. The playmates were glad to be together again. At once they sat down close to each other on the grass, and looked at Gentian's paper.

"What is it that you can't understand?" Aziel whispered, so as not to disturb the other children, who had now gone back to their work.

"Well, it's the words first. What do they mean?"

Now it is not easy for a little girl of Aziel's age to explain the meanings of words, no matter how well she understands them herself. But Aziel tried hard. And here in this bright quiet, Gentian found that the meanings of the words were coming back into her mind all of their own accord anyway.

"Oh, I understand now," she said suddenly. "I see it all. I'd like to try finishing it for myself, I think."

"All right," Aziel agreed. "I'll do mine at the same time, and we can compare answers."

So each little girl bent over her knee, and worked out the problem without help. And when they were done, the answers were the same.

The Teacher came over to look. "Yes, yours are both right," she assured them. "And Gentian has made her figures so round and clear that we might all take a lesson from her! I would be very proud to have you for a pupil of mine!"

How happy Gentian was!

"Oh, I wish I *were* a pupil of yours!" she cried.

"Well, even though you belong in the school down there," the Teacher assured her, "still when things get *too* difficult, you know, you may come up to us, where you can do your best in bright quiet."

"Oh, I shall never dread school again then!"

"We are going to dance now; would you like to stay a while longer and dance too?"

"But I don't know how. Mother hasn't sent us to dancing school."

"Oh, it's not that sort of dancing at all. You shall see. Only stay."

"May we have a circle dance today?" begged Aziel. "Oh, may it be a circle dance?"

The Teacher nodded. All the children then joined hands in a circle. But how shall I tell you of that dance? It was in the Clear Land, you see, and no dancing was ever like it down here.

Gentian's silver sandals helped her a great deal, of course. They were so light, and in the Clear Land they could climb the air, remember.

In a circle, and to the music of the leaves on the vine and of a splashing fountain not far off, the children started dancing. They danced away out of the arbor, over a meadow, tranquil in the crystal light, to the music of a stream that ran through it; then into a wood, and there to the music of bird songs; over a hill to the music of the light spring wind in the long grass; and then up into the blue air—to the music of their own happiness!

Those who were not wearing silver sandals were drawn along and up by those who were. And I think those dancers felt as the wind feels in the spring time when it moves across a cherry orchard, all in blossom.

At last, still in a circle, they came into the arbor again and dropped to rest on the grass.

The Teacher was waiting there. She took Gentian's hand, and bending down to her said, "Your half hour is up, little human. Miss Todd wants you back. Here is your cap."

The dunce cap, which Gentian had forgotten at once on coming into this other school, had fallen off, just as she danced out of the arbor. The Teacher was putting it back on her fairy-gold head now, but smiling so beautifully right down into her eyes as she did it that Gentian did not mind the cap a bit. Then the Teacher turned her around and gave her a gentle push toward—the corner of her own school-room!

And it was well that the dunce cap had been put back, for at that instant Gentian felt another hand on her shoulder, a hand that turned her around. Her eyes were seeing sunlight again, and the four walls of her own schoolroom. It was Miss Todd's hand now on her shoulder. The arbor, the Clear Children, the other Teacher, where were they?

They were there, of course, still. It was only that Gentian

was seeing in sunlight now, not in that other crystal, Clear Light.

"Well, Gentian," Miss Todd was saying, "you may take your seat. And next time, perhaps, you will remember at least to *start* a problem, when I—"

But Miss Todd forgot what she had meant to say in amazement at Gentian's happy, smiling face. Never had she seen a child's face sunnier in all her years of teaching. She had not expected this, of course, from a little girl who had been standing with her face in a corner and a dunce cap on her head for half an hour.

And Gentian's schoolmates were as amazed as Miss Todd was, for there was no understanding it.

But Gentian did not notice their surprise. She was too full of her experience. She looked up at Miss Todd, though, and said, "I have found out how to do that example. I couldn't do it before because I didn't remember what the words meant. But now I have remembered."

"That is well," said Miss Todd, a little doubtfully. "Then you may do it now on the board for the class, explaining it as you do."

And Gentian did take a piece of chalk and work the problem. She remembered what the other Teacher had said about her beautifully formed figures, and now she tried to make these even rounder and clearer than they had been up there. She did the figuring quickly, and explained it well.

And Miss Todd, who was suddenly truly sorry that she had made Gentian wear the dunce cap, said, "Very well done. Very well done, indeed! But you should have told me, Gentian, that you didn't understand the wording of the problem. I would gladly have helped you."

Then came recess and Kay quickly sought his sister out. Standing so that their schoolmates might not see, he squeezed her hand. "Don't you care, Gentian dear," he whispered. "If anybody laughs about the dunce cap or even says a word—well, they'd better not try, that's all!"

Kay's other hand was clenched and his mouth set.

"Thanks, Kay," his sister whispered back, squeezing his hand in turn. "But I didn't mind a bit, not after the first. I'll tell you all about it going home. And oh, please don't fight about me, Kay, no matter what they do! You know how Mother hates your fighting!"

But Kay had no need to fight, for there was not a single jeer, and no one cried, "Oh, see the dunce!" Who would be tempted to mock the happy, confident little girl Gentian had become?

Instead, one little girl called "tag" as she ran by at that minute, touching Gentian lightly on the shoulder; and Gentian whirled away in a noisy game of tag with all the children. But she was not "it" for long, as you must know, for she could run like the wind.

Chapter 10

The Secret Door

THAT night, the family in the little brown house finished their supper before it was time to light the lamps. The world was just turning violet, and the sky dimming.

"We are through early tonight," Detra said. "I shall have a long evening for the Wind Boy. I am going to break him all up, and begin quite over. For I shall never be satisfied with him as he is."

The children were sorry that their mother was going to destroy the statuette. It was so *almost* like the Wind Boy they knew, that they had become more attached to it than to anything their mother had ever made before.

"But if I do him better?" Detra said. "You will be glad then!"

"Be sure you keep him the Wind Boy, though," Kay begged. "He is like that, you know—only more so."

Detra laughed at that, but in her heart she knew that Kay was right. "Yes, I will keep him the same boy," she promised. "Only I will make him truer."

Then she ran upstairs to bring down the statuette.

The children were still at the table, although they had finished their supper.

"Outdoors is getting into purple now," Gentian said. "It's like the Wind Boy's eyes. Let's go out and see if he's in the cherry tree yet." Nan had told them that he watched for the Masker there at twilight.

"All right, let's."

But at that minute came the scratching and rustling at the window that the children remembered. Quickly they turned their faces. Yes, there in the open window showed the mask! The horrid pointed ears, the horrid grin froze their hearts, as always before when they had seen them. They stood, staring.

Would it jump over the sill and rush toward them in the room? It looked as though it might. It was staring straight back at them. Then suddenly Nan opened the door from the kitchen. She was coming in to clear the table. The Masker saw the opening door and dropped down out of sight. They heard its feet racing away, right across Kay's own garden plots.

Kay forgot his terror at that. He sprang up and was away out of the door after the Masker. Gentian stayed behind only the briefest instant, screwing up her courage, and then she too dashed away. Nan, looking after them, smiled, for she had no fear that harm would come to them.

Kay reached the door just in time to glimpse the blue cloak of the Masker whisking away through the hole in the lilac hedge. Mother, of course, did not want the children to

go into the Artist's garden, but Kay very well knew that *this* would make a difference. She would be only too proud of him should he catch the Masker and capture the mask, no matter where he went to do it!

Seen from behind, and while it was running away like this, the Masker was not terrifying at all. Far from it. It was just a slim little figure, no taller than Kay himself, in a blue cape to its heels.

Gentian was through the hole in the hedge almost as soon as Kay, and by the time he had reached the sloping long green terrace running right up to the Artist's front door, she was quite up to him. But the fleeing Masker was far ahead, already on the broad, gravel drive, running for dear life. Well, it must turn about when it reached the house and go in some other direction. Then they would have it. They ran on.

But the Masker did not turn back when it reached the house. No, it dashed on and around a corner, and was lost to the children's eyes.

To their delight now, they heard the whir of wings, and saw the Wind Boy a little way above them, flying fast through the purple twilight.

"Oh splendid! He'll catch it surely," the children thought, and followed on.

But the Wind Boy did not catch the Masker that evening, nor did the children. For a strange thing happened. The Wind Boy had followed around the corner and overtaken the fleeing Masker. He had no thought of failure now and glided to the ground, reaching a hand to seize the mask. Then suddenly the Masker turned about, just escaping his hand, pushed behind a syringa bush that grew against the house, threw open a little low door in the wall, and was gone.

The Wind Boy stopped stock still, amazed. Well he knew that he could never open a door down here in this land. His were a Wind Boy's hands, strong and useful enough in his own Clear Land, but quite helpless with anything so heavy as this door.

When Gentian and Kay came running up, his face was clouded indeed.

"Where did it go?" Kay cried.

"In at the door behind that syringa bush," the Wind Boy said, with deep disgust.

"Right into the house?"

"Yes, right into the house, of course, else I'd have got the mask as last. I never came so near it before."

Kay was troubled. "It'll frighten Rosemarie, then," he cried. "Oh, she'll be terribly frightened!"

Then he turned and ran. The Wind Boy and Gentian had no idea what he meant to do, but they followed to see. Kay was set on doing a very brave thing. He ran around the great house and up the wide, shallow marble steps to the front door. There, standing in the twilight, a determined little boy, he pulled the bell. Gentian and the Wind Boy followed him. They would stand by.

The door was promptly opened by a maid servant. She stared down at Kay, surprised. "What is it? Why do you come to the front door?" she asked with curiosity. A child at the great front door was the last thing she had expected to find.

"Please," said Kay. "That Masker—you know the horrid thing with long ears and a queer mouth—well, it has just now gone right into your house. It will frighten Rosemarie."

The maid squeaked like a frightened mouse, and jumped out beside them. "Then not a step I'll stir back 'till it's out of it again."

"But Rosemarie will be frightened," Kay gasped. "She may be frightened now. You must go to stop that."

I do not know what the maid would have done next had the Policeman at that minute not come up the steps to find what the trouble was about. He had seen the children at the Artist's front door and felt they did not belong there. "What is all this?" he asked, for he had heard Kay's words. "What will frighten Miss Rosemarie?"

"The Masker," Kay answered, turning around, glad now of the Policeman's interference, and not a bit afraid. "It came to our window and we chased it. We followed it right up to the house here and then around to the side. It ran in at a door behind the syringa bush there. The Wind Boy saw it go in at the door."

"There isn't any door behind the syringa bush," said the maid. "You must be dreaming."

"And *who* saw it?" asked the Policeman.

"The Wind Boy. He came flying past us over our heads, and got around the corner first. That is why he was in time to see it go in at the little door."

"Where is the Wind Boy now?"

"Why, right here by Gentian."

The Policeman looked down at Gentian, but he did not see the Wind Boy. His eyes were not nearly clear enough for that.

He stared at Kay and Gentian very suspiciously then. "Come, show us that door," he said gruffly.

"There just isn't any door there at all, so why bother?" snapped the maid. She had begun to get over her fright and to think the children impudent and mischievous. The

Policeman thought them impudent and mischievous too. But he remembered Nan, and the way he had looked through her eyes to the mountains. He hesitated. "I'll give them every chance," he thought then. "That girl certainly thinks they are all right. But nevertheless, there is something very queer about all this."

Out loud he said, "Come, anyway, and we'll make certain about the door."

But Kay cried, "Rosemarie! What about her? Aren't you going to see that she's not being frightened?"

"You're right," said the Policeman then. "If by any chance the Masker did get into the house she may very well be frightened. Better go in, Beta, (Beta was the maid's name) and see that the little girl is safe."

"No indeed, I'll not go a step," said Beta, frightened again, now that she thought the Policeman was taking the children's story seriously.

"What? You afraid of the Masker too? Then I'll have to go with you. And you children, don't move a step from here until we get back. I mean to get to the bottom of this. Indeed, it's more my duty than ordinary, since the Artist is away."

The great door closed, and the children waited. They had no temptation to go away. They were only too eager to stay and learn whether the Masker was caught. The Wind Boy was on tiptoes with excitement. The three sat down on the lowest marble step, until the great door should open again.

But it was a long time before the door opened. The Artist's house was a very, very big one indeed, and there were many rooms, corners, passages and closets into which the Policeman had to look to make sure that the Masker was not hiding. He was rather cross when at last he did come out, for against his reason he had hoped to get his hands on the Masker at last, and so win the Artist's praise and reward, when he should come home tomorrow.

"Well, youngsters," he said shortly, "come now and show me that wonderful door that probably isn't a door at all. Miss Rosemarie is busy at her lessons, safe and quiet, as you would be if your mother took proper care of you, and kept you out of mischief, evenings. Where are you anyway?"

For he did not see them just at first in their place on the low step.

But Kay had jumped up. "Our mother does take proper care of us," cried Kay. "We just followed the Masker to catch it, that was all. She would want us to do that."

"Likely enough," answered the Policeman, striding down the steps. "But step lively now, and show us that door."

So Gentian and Kay and the Wind Boy led the way around the house to the syringa bush. Of course Beta and the Policeman could not see the Wind Boy, although it was his hands that parted the sweet-smelling white blossoms that brushed the hidden door. The Policeman and Beta thought it was just a little wind stirring on the edge of night that did it. But even when the flowers were parted, they could not see the door. Even Kay and Gentian could not see the door.

Kay and Gentian were startled. Had the Wind Boy made a mistake? And what would the Policeman think about that? Oh, he would mistrust them more than ever now! He would think they had lied. They were troubled indeed.

But the Wind Boy said, "Push against the wall right here. That's all the Masker did, and it opened just as easy."

Kay thought it would be too silly to push against the wall where the Wind Boy was pointing; it seemed so much like all the rest of the wall there, just wall, without a sign of a door.

The Policeman could not hear the Wind Boy's voice. He only thought to himself, "The wind is rising a little." He began to laugh, not a very pleasant laugh, for now he thought he had found the children out. They were truly, in his words, "bold ones and mischief-makers."

But Gentian stepped forward and did as the Wind Boy said. She pushed against the blank wall with all her strength. And the next she knew, she was lying flat on her face in a very dark place. There had been no need to push so hard, for the door opened at a touch!

But she was not hurt a bit. Up she jumped and stood alone in the pitch dark, for the door had swung to behind her. But now that those outside knew that there was a door, they pushed it open again and let her out.

"Well, I never," Beta gasped, poking her head in at the

door that was now held open by the Policeman. "I never heard of such a thing at all. And who'd ever guess it? Why, there's just nothing to show!"

The Policeman was as surprised as Beta.

"It's a secret door," he said. "That's what it is. We'll have to see where it leads."

"Why, it's just the coat closet under the back stairs," Beta exclaimed, craning her neck. "A body coming in could run right up the back stairs and be seen by nobody."

"Well then, I shall just have to ask the Artist when he returns whether he knows about this door," the Policeman said importantly. "And you, Beta, please say nothing about it."

"But my master won't be back until tomorrow," Beta cried. "Until then, am I to sleep in a house with a secret door and not even a key in it, and say nothing to nobody?"

"Yes, that is just what you are to do. And, you children, you too, say nothing."

The children nodded. It was very exciting, and surely very important to be sharing a secret with the Policeman.

But at that minute: "Gentian! Kay! Time to come in. Gentian! Kay!" Nan was standing in the doorway of the little brown house calling them.

"So they *are* looking out for you after all," said the Policeman, but not gruffly now. "I'm glad to know it. But I might have trusted that girl to have an eye out for you, anyway! *She'd* know where you were!"

He meant Nan. In all his life he was never to forget her

and the far-off mountains he had seen through her clear eyes.

"Are you coming with us, Wind Boy? Do," whispered Gentian.

But the Wind Boy shook his head. "No," he said. "I'm going to stay around by this door to make sure the Masker doesn't come out. Oh, if I had only caught it!"

So Gentian and Kay had to run home without him, for Nan was calling again.

When they had gone, the Policeman said to Beta: "You'd better go in too, or the other maids will be asking you all sorts of questions. I shall stay here a bit to think things over."

Beta went, reluctant and grumbling, but not daring to disobey the Policeman. Then the Policeman sat down in front of the syringa bush to do his thinking of things over at his ease. But his eyes were alert and keen enough as they rested on the hidden door, in spite of all his puzzling thoughts. Beside him, waiting too and watching, sat the Wind Boy, cross-legged, his purple wings folded down his back.

But the Policeman knew nothing of the Wind Boy. Now and then he did hear the rustle of the Wind Boy's wings, as he changed his position a little. But if he thought about the sound at all, it was to him just the night wind among the syringa flowers.

So the purple twilight fell deeper and deeper all around them, until they were just the faintest outlines in the dusk.

But as the purple deepened, the Policeman, staying on

so stolidly there in the gathering dew, forgot to puzzle about the Masker and the secret door. He had fallen to thinking about Nan instead—that strange girl who had come to work for the foreigners in the little brown house. It is not every day you can see far-off purple mountains just by looking into a girl's clear eyes!

And the Wind Boy was thinking about Gentian. What a brave little girl she had been to run after the Masker! Kay was brave, of course. Boys had to be. But Gentian was brave because she had promised to help him, the Wind Boy! He was sure of that.

So the Policeman and the Wind Boy thought their thoughts without interfering with each other, in the purple twilight, on watch at the secret door.

Chapter 11

Gentian at the Loom

WHEN the children got back to the little brown house they found their mother beside the lamp and the bowl of tulips, working with the plastilina. Already it was beginning to take shape again.

They stopped by her shoulder to watch. She hardly knew that they were there, however, she was so absorbed in what she was doing. And because they wanted the work to go well just as much as she did, and because they knew that if they spoke and called her mind away, she might do no more that night, they said not a word, but after a little, quietly turned aside. Kay settled down to a book he was reading, a story of the sea. And Gentian ran softly up to Nan's attic room.

Nan was sitting in the open window, mending one of Kay's stockings. Beside her was a heap of brown and black stockings belonging to both the children, and a torn frock of Gentian's. Nan was holding her work close to the window to catch the very last ray of light.

She looked up at Gentian, and smiled a greeting. She knew very well what Gentian wanted, for each night that Nan had been here Gentian had come up to look at, and touch, the starry-brightness nightrobe.

So now Nan said, even before Gentian had asked permission: "Yes. You may open the drawer and take it out."

"Oh, and may I bring it over there by the window?"

"Yes, do."

So Gentian pulled out the top drawer in the chest of drawers; and that, to her, was something like opening a door into the night sky—the nightrobe lay folded there so blue and starry.

Gentian lifted it out with her fingertips. She had to look to make sure that there was anything there but air, it was so light! Slowly, and careful that its trailing, wisping folds should not sweep the floor, she carried it over to the window, and the last light of day. There she sat down on the floor at Nan's knee and held the wonderful robe in her lap. Her face, as she bent above it, was full of delight and wonder.

Nan put by her darning to watch Gentian's face, so full of rapture. But Gentian was too lost in the happiness of gazing at the starry-brightness to know that Nan was looking at her. At last, in spite of her delight, she sighed, but ever so softly.

"What is it, Gentian?" Nan asked in words almost as soft as the sigh.

"Oh, I wonder if I shall ever have anything so beautiful!"

Nan did not answer at once, but stayed looking down into Gentian's lifted blue eyes. Then she said in a matter-of-fact voice, "Anyone who has a nightgown like this has to make it, Gentian. I do not know whether you could learn to make it, but I think you *might!*"

"But where would I ever get the starry-brightness to make it of?"

"Why, you would have to make that starry-brightness. That is what I meant."

"Well, I could hardly do that."

"Why do you say so? Wouldn't you like to try?"

"How could I try?"

"Trying is the easiest end of it. It is the doing that will tell."

Gentian was gazing up at Nan with hope and delight now in her blue eyes.

"If you want to try right away, now, tonight, you will have to go through into the other house, the one above this one. Remember? For the starry-brightness cannot be made down here, not without giving a lifetime to it!"

"Do you mean that little brown house we saw just above ours in the crystal light that day with the Wind Boy? I am to go up there?"

"Yes. A young woman who lives in that house has promised me that she will help you with the making of a little starry-brightness robe just for yourself. This morning, when I was tidying my room, I suddenly saw the way up into that other house. There I found her, and we talked about you and the way you came at night to see my starry

robe. And she herself said she would ask the Great Artist—
their Great Artist, you know—to set up his loom for you.
She is expecting you now."

"Oh, how kind she is! But what has the Great Artist to
do with it?"

"He has the loom and the colors. So it is to his house
you must go, if you are to weave the starry-brightness. Run
through now to the other house and the kind young girl
will take you."

Gentian sprang up, and ran to put Nan's nightrobe
back in the drawer. Then she looked all about the little attic room eagerly, expectantly. But slowly her eager face
grew blank. "Oh, where can I go through?" she cried. "See
Nan, it is all just a hard old plaster wall!"

"You will have to get very still, and then remember what
the Wind Boy showed us when he pointed. That is all."

So Gentian grew very still. She even shut her eyes. And
she remembered—hard.

"Are you through?" Nan asked after a minute.

"Why, no," said Gentian, when she had opened her
eyes and glanced about at the attic room, very dim now in
the dusk. "Can't you see I'm still here?"

"Well, *I'm* through," Nan laughed. "And I couldn't
know whether you were too, without asking, could I!"

"You're through! Through to the other house!"

"Yes."

"But that can't be. You're here with me."

"I am through at the same time. And I do wish you

would hurry and come too, for I must get back to those stockings. There are so many, and Kay needs his for school tomorrow."

Gentian was almost in tears. She believed Nan when she said that she was through into the Clear Land, although she could not understand how that could be, when she saw her here at the same time. But there was something in Nan's voice and in her eyes that made everyone who listened to her and looked at her believe her, no matter how strange a thing she said. "But what can I do to come through, too?" Gentian begged.

"Grow still."

"I am still."

"I don't mean that kind of still, still with your body. I mean deep-still, still with your heart!"

So Gentian tried again. But how was she ever to grow deep-still when she was so excited!

"Deep-still. Deep-still. Deep-still," Nan said to her, softly over and over. And when Nan's voice stopped, Gentian *had* grown deep-still. And there she was, through into the other house!

She was standing with Nan in an attic room very like Nan's own. Only, even at first glance, you would have known it was a room in the Clear Land. For the light was clearest, serenest crystal; and though it was almost night here, as in the land below, there was no darkness in this twilight—the purple dusk was bathed in crystal.

"I can't stay with you because of the stockings," Nan

said. "But if you run down the stairs you will find that kind young girl waiting for you somewhere, I am sure. I told her you would come, you know."

"Oh, please, do stay," Gentian begged.

When she had gone up into the Clear Land with Kay and the Wind Boy, she had felt no strangeness, and when she had got through to the other school, she had not felt strange either. But here, in the Clear Land's dusk, in its purple shadows (even if they were crystal shadows!), in this empty attic room, she did feel strange and alone. "Please stay," she begged.

Nan shook her head. "No, I must go back. But run along down, dear, and bring back with you, if you can, a starry-brightness nightrobe."

At mention of the starry-brightness nightrobe Gentian forgot her strangeness. She stood on tiptoe to kiss Nan's cheek, and then without another word she ran out of the room and down the stairs.

In her own house the stairs would have been quite dark by now. But here in this other house, she could see well enough in the shadows. She went rather shyly through the hall downstairs, to the sitting-room door. For after all this house that she had entered from the top was not her own, and she had not even knocked!

But the sitting room was empty. How like, and how unlike their own! There was the big bowl of tulips on a little low table against the wall! Only the curtains were golden, not brown. For a minute she thought that she must be dreaming, or that she was still in her own house, after all. But as she stood there alone for a minute, the crystal light and a sweet stillness over everything made her know that she was indeed in the Clear Land.

But where was the friendly young girl Nan had promised would be waiting? The strangeness had come back to Gentian's heart as she stood alone in this other room. She turned and very softly, lonelily, went out into the hall and to the door.

There on the doorstep in the crystal, lonely twilight sat a girl, about Nan's age, a girl with a clear, quiet face. Twilight was in her eyes and in her hair, and she was wrapped about in a twilight cloak. Gentian never learned her name, but then, and always after, she called her the "Twilight Girl."

"I was waiting for you," said the Twilight Girl. "Nan was sure you would want to come. I have told the Artist, and he has set up the colors and left the loom ready."

Gentian clapped her hands. "Thank you, oh thank you. If I *can* only make a starry-brightness nightrobe like Nan's!"

"Come then," the Twilight Girl said, rising and taking Gentian by the hand. They went out at the little swinging gate, down the street, and turned in at the Artist's drive. Looking up at the mansion, Gentian saw how it was very like their own Artist's mansion—except that it was whiter and more shining—and its towers and arches were lost in the sky.

Up the wide, shallow marble steps they went and in at the great front door, which was standing wide open. The Twilight Girl had not bothered to ring the bell, nor did she now look around for anyone. She led Gentian in as though the house were hers, and up the stairway.

At first Gentian felt a little shy about coming into the Great Artist's house so. But then she remembered how Nan had told Detra that children were free to go in and out of the Great Artist's house just as the wind was free to blow in and out—and she felt strange about it no longer.

Up and up and up they went, flight after flight of wide stairs, and at the top of each flight, through winding passages. If Gentian had climbed so many stairs down in the world, her legs would surely have begun to ache. But here her sandals were silver, remember, and it was rather like climbing blue air. Indeed, the stairs were blue, and may very well have been air.

Down one long passage, she saw the Great Artist himself, pacing back and forth before a row of windows, opening toward the twilight mountains. He was very tall and very noble, and dressed in a flowing, silvery robe. His head was bent as he paced, or turned away toward the windows; and so he did not see Gentian and the Twilight Girl, or know that they had stopped to gaze at him.

"He is planning his work," the Twilight Girl whispered.

And Gentian remembered how her mother, when she was planning a new statue, would pace back and forth in the same way.

After that they climbed a very steep, narrow flight of stairs that ended in a tower room.

The windows all around were opened outward, and when Gentian stood in the room she felt that she was standing high up in the sky, where it turns to blue. Only now it was the soft blue of evening.

By one of the windows a little loom was set up, and before it stood a stool.

"Sit here on the stool," the Twilight Girl said, "and I will show you how to begin."

So Gentian sat down on the stool before the loom. Her feet did not touch the floor, and the Twilight Girl smiled at that. "You are, after all, a very little girl to be sitting at this loom," she said. "But it will do no harm to try, and Nan thought you could make the starry-brightness—even if your feet wouldn't touch!"

How grateful Gentian was to Nan for so believing in her! And when the Twilight Girl had shown her how to handle the colors and how to set to work, she said to herself, "Oh, it's much easier than I thought it could be. I know I can do it."

"Now," the Twilight Girl said, giving all the colors into her hands, "try."

But Gentian hardly had to try. She could do it right from the first. Very swiftly under her hands, starry-brightness began to grow. And very soon she found that as she worked she could think, too. And she went on thinking her thoughts while her hands flew.

She thought: "Oh, this is going to be too beautiful to wear at night when no one sees me! I want to wear it in the day. When my classmates down there see me coming, in something so beautiful and strange, they will not laugh at me any more. They will stop talking about my being so queer, and a foreigner. They will wish that *they* had a starry-brightness, and talk only about that."

But as Gentian thought these thoughts, the threads had grown tangled, and more tangled, until now they ended in a snarl, and the starry-brightness was losing its starriness under her fingers.

"What are you doing?" wondered the Twilight Girl bending above her. "What are you thinking of to let the stars go!"

Then Gentian told her what she was thinking of. The Twilight Girl shook her head. "That was it," she said, her smile a little sad. "Of course you can't weave the starry robe with those thoughts! Starry-brightness is not to make you proud before others with; it is just for yourself. You can't make it, except just for yourself."

"Do you mean that my thoughts spoil it?" asked Gentian, surprised.

"Of course," answered the Twilight Girl. "You must give up wanting *anybody* to see your robe, and then you may be able to untangle the threads, perhaps."

So Gentian gave up the thought, and the threads almost untangled themselves in her fingers.

Again the weaving went on, swiftly and smoothly. And soon it was going so easily, that Gentian began to think her thoughts again. As it grew in beauty and starriness, she thought: "Oh, I want Mother to have one. Darling Mother, who works so hard and has no pretty clothes. How happy such a beautiful starry robe would make her! I would rather she had it than I!"

But the threads were getting tangled again, and the stars no longer forming.

"What are you thinking of now?" the Twilight Girl spoke softly, bending at Gentian's shoulder. "Something is wrong. See, there are no more stars."

Gentian told her thoughts. The Twilight Girl's smile was not sad now. But it was grave. "That was a nice thought, Gentian," she said. "But this kind of a robe each one must make for oneself. No one can do it for another. You must make it yours in your thought, or it will not come right."

That saddened Gentian for a minute. Where was the happiness in doing it just for yourself, if you couldn't do it for someone else too? But after a minute her doubt about the happiness of it passed, and she tried again.

Then the stars came quickly and flowingly, and the blue, under Gentian's flying fingers, trembled and grew deep into a sky.

And Gentian thought: "It isn't every little girl of eight who could make a thing so beautiful! I must be different somehow from most other children——"

But hardly had the stars at this thought begun to dim, before, without noticing, she stopped. "No, no," she said out loud. "It was the Artist who set up the loom for me,

and gave me the colors. I must be grateful to the Artist. He could do it for any little girl he wanted to!"

And the Twilight Girl, who had reached a hand to stop Gentian, drew it back now, a light of gladness in her eyes.

After that, the starry robe grew and grew. Sometimes, with her thoughts, the threads would go wrong again and begin to tangle. But then Gentian would rest a minute and get deep-still. After that her thoughts would change, and all would be well.

And soon those times ended altogether, and it was smooth work, and swift.

The starry-brightness had grown almost large enough now for a nightrobe for Gentian, and it lay on the loom like a piece of the night sky.

It was then that the Great Artist came up the narrow steep stairs into the tower room, and stood behind Gentian, looking down at her busy fingers. But Gentian had not heard him, so softly had he come. The Twilight Girl stood back, so that he might see all. He nodded and then stayed still, watching.

Soon, all the thread was used, and Gentian turned to look up at the Twilight Girl. When she saw the Great Artist above her there in his silvery robes, she got down from the stool, and stood before him, awed and happy.

"You have done well, little human," he said in a voice the sound of which Gentian could never afterward remember.

Perhaps Gentian should have thanked him then for

having set up the loom for her, and letting her come up to work on it. But she was too much in awe of him to say anything at all! She could only smile up into his deep eyes, and be still. Then he stooped, and taking the starry-brightness from the loom, handed it to her. She gazed her thanks out of her blue-gentian eyes, as she held the starry-brightness against her breast. The Twilight Girl took her hand and led her away down the stairs.

When they got back to the little brown house, the Twilight Girl said gently: "Run up the stairs now, Gentian, and back to Nan, who is waiting. It will be easy enough for you to find the way through to the Earth with that starry robe in your arms. Everything will be easier."

She bent down and kissed Gentian on her cheek (a cool, kind kiss). "The Great Artist was pleased with you. You should be very happy," she said.

"I am very, very happy!" Gentian answered. "And oh, I thank you."

The Twilight Girl shook her head, smiling. "You did it all—every bit, yourself. Nan will know!"

So Gentian ran away up the stairs. And when she opened the door into the attic room she knew that she was back in her own world. For there was dark at the window, and Nan was sitting by a lamp, finishing the last stocking.

Gentian ran to her and threw the starry-brightness, in a heap, into her lap. How Nan's face shone then! Yes, I think it outshone even Gentian's.

"Now, I will sew it up for you," she said, "and tonight you shall sleep in it."

"Oh, will you? And may I?" Gentian clapped her hands.

So, under the lamp light, Nan sewed up the starry, filmy gown, while Gentian knelt on the floor at her knee, and watched. When it was done she handed it to Gentian and said: "Now run away to bed before your mother remembers to send you. That will be a fine surprise for her."

For once in her life Gentian was only too eager to run away to bed.

Chapter 12

On Paths of Night

THERE was no need of a lamp in the room to undress by, for the stars had risen, and the room was silvery with their shining. Gentian's nightrobe, by star shine, was even lovelier than it had been by lamp light. The stars in it had a clearer radiance, and the blue quivered in a light all its own. The minute that Gentian had slipped out of her clothes, and into this loveliness, she felt that she had become as light as the gown. "Light as a feather!" she thought. But then she knew at once that that was not right–she was lighter than a feather. For a feather must sometime flutter to the earth, but she felt that if she were to leave the ground, she could stay in the air as long as ever she liked.

"Oh, how wonderful! How wonderful!" she thought. Of course she had climbed the air very lately in the Clear Country. But in that crystal land, it did not seem like such a marvelous thing to do. Here, in her mother's little brown house, right down here in the village where she lived, to climb the air would be a different, stranger thing.

Gentian got onto the one chair in the bedroom to gaze at herself in her mother's high mirror. The nightrobe looked like a blue cloud fallen about her, and the stars in it shone out softly radiant, lighting her hair and face. She got down from the chair and went to the door, which she quietly opened. After hesitating there a minute, she went down the stairs. She stood in the doorway of the sitting room, looking at her mother and Kay, a merry laugh ready to break on her lips, when they should see her there in her glimmering nightrobe. She wanted to watch the wonder grow in their eyes.

But Detra was bent over the statuette, her eyes narrowed, while her hands worked cleverly and quickly, making the Wind Boy's clustering curls. Her thoughts were all on her work, and she had forgotten where she was, even perhaps, who she was. As for Kay, he sat beyond her, at the other side of the table, to get the lamp light too. His coppery head was bent over his book, and his eyes, following the pages, never wavered. He was far out at sea on a sailing vessel, lost in another world, another time.

Gentian stood watching her mother and her brother for some minutes. But they did not look or sense that she was there. She could not get Kay's attention, of course, without disturbing her mother. And now that she saw how her mother was working, with the intent, narrowed eyes that Gentian knew so well, she dared not disturb her. Her heart sank a little, for she had longed to show them her handiwork.

But after a little waiting there unnoticed in the doorway, she quietly turned and went back up the stairs to her room. Well, in the morning she could show them. She would go to bed now. So she turned back the bedclothes and, after kneeling to say her bedtime prayer, got in.

At once she fell asleep. But it was not in the way she, or any other little girl, usually falls asleep. The minute her head touched the pillow, she felt herself slipping into sleep as into deep water. Only of course sleep did not take her breath away as water will when your head goes under. When her head went under in this water of sleep, her breath came lighter and lighter, easier and easier—until, it was not like breathing at all, it was so light. And then she forgot everything, she thought of nothing. Of course she could never tell about that. That was the very deepest sleep a person can know.

And the next minute she was wide awake!

She had slept only the briefest while. But because it had been so deep a sleep, and so dreamless, it had rested her more than a whole night of just ordinary every-night sleep. Now she was suddenly wide awake, wider awake than she had ever been in her life perhaps, here in her bed with the starlight pouring in at the window.

She sat up. Only it was not like sitting up at all, for she came up as lightly as the tulips had come up after the Wind Boy had run over them. And then she noticed that every movement she made was made as she thought it—as though her thoughts did the moving, and not her body at all. That was delightful. Thinking it, she got out of bed and went to the door.

"Why, this is the way the clouds move, and the wind!" she thought. She went down the stairs as a petal floats from the cherry tree. And in a second she was standing on the grass, in the lamp light, just outside the sitting-room window.

She crossed her arms on the sill and looked in. Oh, if they would only look up and see her now. How amazed they would be! The Masker had stood like this, looking in, and just at first they might think *she* was the Masker. But right away they would know better, and Kay would laugh.

But what would her mother say to her being out alone in the night? Well, Gentian knew very well that ordinarily her mother would not like it at all, that she would never allow her to do such a thing. But in this nightrobe that made her so light, in this starry-brightness, everything was different. Her mother would surely be wise enough to see that. Why, in this starry-brightness, she was *part* of the night, she was the sky itself, and the night wind! She belonged out here!

Detra and Kay worked and read on, and never dreamed that Gentian was out there in the night, looking in at them. After a little she turned away and moved like a cloud across the little grass plot, through the hole in the hedge, down the grassy paths to the stone steps that led up to the tulip garden.

In the tulip garden, in the grassy center where the Wind

Boy had slept, Gentian sat with her arms wrapped about her knees. She stayed that way for a long time, getting stiller and stiller. "I'm still the way the night is still," she told herself. But after some while longer she began to feel how alone she was out here, how far from her mother and Kay, back there under the lamp light in the little brown house! And as she looked toward the little brown house, she saw Nan's light wink out in the attic. Was Nan in her starry-brightness too, and would she come out into the soft night?

Gentian thought of the Wind Boy. Why had she and Kay, Saturday morning, run away to play with the Clear Children and left him behind? Well, she would not play with the Clear Children again, unless they would let him play, too.

But they must find the Masker. Tomorrow night at dusk they must do nothing but watch. And when they did catch it, and the Wind Boy had torn off the mask—how splendid for them all it would be! The Wind Boy would be happy again. He would look as he had looked that minute when he first awoke, here at noon, while Gentian was watching him. He would measure for silver sandals then, and the Shoeman would be glad. He could go back to play with the Clear Children and be at home once again in the Clear Land. And Gentian and Kay would play with him there, and with the others.

And once the Wind Boy was happy, Mother could make her statuette look happy too, and ready to fly with *all of him*. For she would see him like that, once he was happy, and free of all that mask business. She would make him glad of his wings, and she would get the light across his brow.

Well, perhaps the Masker was hiding somewhere out here, perhaps in that black shadow over there by the white birch at the edge of the garden!

Gentian looked hard, but could see nothing, so velvet-black was the shadow. Yes, the Masker might very well be there—yet she was not a bit afraid at the thought. In her starry-brightness she could not be afraid of anything so foolish and silly as that mask! Indeed, she could not remember now how it was that such a silly thing had *ever* frightened her.

She turned her back on the velvet shadow. But her

courage was not needed. The Masker was not lurking there. If the moonlight and starlight could have sifted through the leaves of the white birch, Gentian would have seen nothing but tulips, red, yellow, purple and white, with their petals closed in the dew.

Gentian now was looking toward the Artist's house. And she thought of Rosemarie, alone, asleep in her high nursery. What fun it would be if she and Kay could only have her for a playmate! But hadn't the Artist half promised it Saturday morning—here in the tulip garden? If when he came back, he should have forgotten, Gentian decided to remind him. For out here in her starry-brightness, she saw how horrid it must be for Rosemarie, always alone. All the tulip gardens in the world, and automobiles and pretty dresses, and famous grandfathers, wouldn't make up to a little girl for being alone. "I will be brave, and speak to the Artist about it," she promised herself.

Then she looked off over the wood to the far-away mountains. They were as black and velvety as the shadow under the white birch.

"Nan came from the mountains," Gentian remembered. "Perhaps she has gone back there now, in her starry-brightness, for a night visit. I shall go and look for her there."

Then she rose and went toward the mountains. She went right across the tulip beds, not bothering about the grassy paths, just as the Wind Boy had done. But that was all right, for the tulips did not even bend under her feet.

I cannot tell you about her journey, through air and

starlight, toward the mountains; for I have never run along the paths of night. Even Gentian herself never found words to tell it in. But she did come to the mountains, moving with her thought, and stood at the top of the very tallest one, just above the spruce and pine and birch trees, on a ragged ledge of gray, moss-covered rock.

The village, as she looked back and down on it, was just a few pinpoints of light. But the sky was close. "Oh, I want to know all about the stars," Gentian thought. "Perhaps Nan can tell me. I shall ask her tomorrow, or tonight if I find her here. How many, many worlds there must be! I want to go to all of them, and live in all of them, one after another, sometime!"

Above the mountaintop just beyond, a light, that was not starlight, suddenly caught her glance. It was moving toward her along the paths of air. Gentian caught her breath, for she thought it might be Nan coming in her starry-brightness. She stood waiting, watching. Slowly it came on toward her through the starlight and the blue. And when it had come quite near, she saw that, although it was someone, it was not Nan. It was much too tall, and she knew that Nan, even in her starry-brightness, could never have just this clear, steady radiance.

Gentian, standing there on her stony ledge on the mountaintop, became stiller than she had ever been in her life before. Yes, stiller than deep-still. Her breath stopped, her heart beat softly; it was as though she hardly lived. She stood straight and still with folded hands, and her eyes stayed open only because she dared not move her lids to cover them.

The Being passed very near her mountaintop, moving slowly, as to unheard holy music. He passed by. But as he passed, he turned his face, and looked down at Gentian, standing still and small on the mountain top.

At his look, she covered her eyes with her hands, and sank down on the moss-covered rock. She lay curled there, remembering brightness and beauty, lost in awe.

But the face itself she never remembered. For it was not a face for a human child to see. When at last she looked up again, the bright Being had passed by, and was gone. It had passed behind the farthest mountain.

For a minute, Gentian wanted to follow, to catch a glimpse again, if only from afar off. She took a step out into the air.

But something stopped her. Perhaps it was the memory of her mother and Kay—or, even more, of her father back there, searching for his family, somewhere in the everyday world. Whatever it was, it turned her about sharply, and sent her running fast along the paths of night toward the pinpoints of light that were the village and home.

When she reached the tulip garden and floated down onto the grassy center, she saw that the little brown house was dark. Mother must have finished with the Wind Boy, and Kay with his book, and both had gone to bed. But where would Mother think Gentian had vanished to, when she saw her bed empty? Gentian had not thought of

Mother's being frightened by her adventure. She ran up the air, and across to her mother's open window. When she stood in the still, shadowy room, she was glad to be there.

How it had happened that Detra, when she came to bed, had failed to notice that Gentian was not there in her own little bed, I cannot tell you. But she had not noticed, surely, or she would not be sleeping peacefully now. Gentian listened to her even, gentle breathing.

"I can never sleep in this starry-brightness," she thought, as she stood glimmering in the room. "It is too wonderful for just a little girl."

So quietly, not to disturb her sleeping mother, she slipped it off, and feeling for her plain, little cotton nightgown on its peg in the dark closet, she put it on instead. Then, still moving very softly, she folded up the starry-brightness and put it away in the lowest empty drawer of her closet. When she closed the drawer, she felt that she was closing a door into the sky.

But it was so still in the house, and she felt so strange and lonely, she could not get into her own bed now and go to sleep. The memory of the brightness and beauty of that face that had turned toward her on the mountain top, and the way she had almost gone after it beyond the mountains, was too keen.

Softly, uncertainly, she stole across and stood beside her mother's bed in the farthest shadow in the room. She bent and touched her mother's cheek with her own.

"Who is that?" Detra asked in a half-asleep voice. "Who?"

"It's Gentian," Gentian whispered, and crept in beside her.

Detra turned and folded an arm about her little girl.

"Why, you are cold!" she whispered. "Snuggle close."

"Oh, may I stay and sleep here?"

"Yes, but why? I thought you were so fast asleep!"

"No, I was out in the night. It was so big! And then came the Angel. I wanted you!"

Detra smiled sleepily to herself in the dark. "What strange dreams you have," she murmured. Then she lay thinking about her little girl and wondering about her for a long time.

But Gentian had fallen asleep almost at once, folded securely in her mother's arms.

Chapter 13

Kay and the Masker

THE next afternoon Kay and Gentian took their home-
work out under the cherry tree. There was more than
usual of it today, and they wanted to get it all out of the way
before twilight. For at twilight, they had promised each
other to lie in wait for the Masker; and they hoped that the
Wind Boy would come to join them. Even as they studied
they kept glancing up, half expecting to see him standing in
the garden waiting for them; and several times Gentian was
sure she spied a bit of his purple wings, when the spring
wind moved overhead in the cherry tree.

"You really must study, Gentian," Kay at last cried, a little impatiently. "If you keep looking up there for him all
the time, and thinking about him, you'll never get done
this afternoon. Then Mother'll keep us in tonight."

Gentian sighed. "All right," she said, "I'll try." And she
bent over her lesson book determinedly.

Just then the Wind Boy did come running down from
the Clear Land and into the boughs of the cherry tree. But

he made no more sound than the spring wind had already made there, so the children did not let themselves look up. He knelt in a forked branch watching them for some time, but they did not lift their eyes from their books. He shook the boughs then, making the air sweet with cherry-blossom smell. Still they did not look.

He spread his purple wings, and drifted to the grass, and standing directly before them, looked down, wistfully, at the coppery tops of their bent heads. He had come to play with them.

But if you are to play with a Wind Boy, you must first see him; and he has no way of getting your attention unless you are quite ready to give it. So he waited now in vain for his human playmates.

At last, too proud to stay longer unwanted, he turned away and flew slowly over the hedge and back to the Artist's tulip garden. There he stretched himself out in the grassy center where the sun was warmest, and stayed half asleep waiting for twilight and time to watch for the Masker.

But back under the cherry tree, it was Gentian who was now nagging Kay. "Really, Kay, unless you stop staring up at that nursery window, you'll never get done, and Mother won't let us out in the twilight! Please!"

You see, Rosemarie had come to her high nursery window, and stood looking down at the brother and sister. She was hoping that Kay would soon stop working at stupid lessons and start climbing. For if she herself might not climb up the brown limbs of that old cherry tree among the budding blossoms, the next best thing was to watch somebody else doing it. But today, alas, he did not climb. And Rosemarie, as the Wind Boy, turned away after a while, lonely and disappointed.

After that, Kay and Gentian got along better with the work that must come before play.

The Wind Boy didn't wait for twilight that night but came back almost as soon as the people in the little brown house were through with supper. Gentian and Kay were out in the yard tossing a ball back and forth to each other, calling and laughing. The Wind Boy heard their happy voices before he came to the hedge.

Gentian was the first to see him. "Oh, you've come," she cried. "We've been looking and looking for you. But it's not time to watch for the Masker yet. What shall we play till twilight?"

She knew very well, of course, that the Wind Boy would not be able to catch or throw their ball; for she remembered that he could not even open the secret door that needed only a touch. In the Clear Land, you must know, the Wind Boy could open doors well enough and play ball too. It was only down here that he had no touch for things.

"Let's play hide-and-seek," he suggested. "I'll count first."

Hide-and-seek was a fine idea.

The Wind Boy faced the cherry tree and, crossing his

arms on the old brown trunk, shut his eyes against them. Away Gentian ran, almost before he had begun to count— around the house, and out across the meadow at the back. There, in a hollow, behind some huckleberry bushes she crouched to hide.

But Kay had not gone so far. He wanted to get his goal and fool the Wind Boy, who he thought must have heard Gentian running away around the house and would go in that direction, leaving him safe to slip in and get "free."

So, very softly, moving on his toes, he got to the lilac hedge, and worked his way in among the bushes. Once there, safely hidden, he stood erect.

The Wind Boy did just as Kay had expected. When he had finished counting, he turned about and looked all around, carefully. For an instant he looked straight at Kay's hiding place, and Kay felt that their eyes met. But they had- n't, for the Wind Boy turned away suddenly and ran in the direction Gentian had taken.

Now Kay would have jumped from his hiding place, and got his goal, but he heard a sound behind him. He turned to see what it was, and stayed completely still. For there, standing close against a tree trunk on the Artist's lawn, and looking back around it, as though in fear of someone's seeing it from the windows of the big house, was the Masker!

It had come early tonight. Kay wanted to shout for the Wind Boy and Gentian. But that would do no good, he knew, for the Masker would only escape again. Then he remembered the Policeman who was to keep special watch every evening. He looked out from his leafy hiding place toward the street. Yes, there was the Policeman just arriving for duty. But Kay did not call to him.

No, he suddenly decided to catch the Masker for himself, and have all the fun of waving the mask in the faces of the Wind Boy and Gentian, when they came running back to the goal.

It would take a little courage, but not too much. The cape the Masker wore had a peaked hood, and the mask, stuck in under such an innocent-looking little hood, was really more comical than dreadful. The Masker really should wait for the twilight to deepen if it wanted to frighten people. But Kay didn't let himself laugh out loud for that would have scared the Masker away.

After a minute the Masker left the concealment of the tree and ran, just as fast as it could, toward the hole in the hedge. To reach the hole, it had to pass Kay. He jumped out and grabbed at the flying cape. With a startled but stifled scream, the Masker wrenched the cape from his grasp and dashed back across the grass, right toward the Artist's house. This time it did not stop to hide behind the trees, for Kay was after it.

Right at once he realized that the Masker was making for the secret door behind the syringa bush. Well, that should not happen again—not if he could help it!

He ran faster than he had known he could run, taking a short cut right across a bed of jonquils. That headed the

Masker off before it could get near the syringa bush. It swerved off, and sped away in the direction of the tulip garden.

Down long grassy paths it ran, its cape billowing out behind it. But Kay was gaining.

And then the Masker stopped bothering about the paths, and dashed through flower beds, over ferns, over fresh-planted places, and at last reached the foot of the stone steps leading up to the tulip garden.

And Kay followed through everything. To what his mother or the Artist would say about the ruin their feet were making he gave not a thought at that time. He was after the Masker, and he meant to catch it. He could only think of that.

Just at the top of the steps the Masker tripped over its cape and fell, sprawling. Kay, who was close behind, and had not time to stop, tripped over the Masker and fell sprawling, too.

Up got the Masker to its knees to run again, but Kay got a good clutch on the hem of its cape, and that was the end, for the cape was fastened securely by a strong hook at the neck.

"There!" cried Kay, springing up. "Now I've got you! You horrid thing that scares children and keeps the Wind Boy away from his comrades. *I'm* not afraid of you!" And he reached for the mask to tear it off. But the Masker itself pulled down the mask before Kay could. And Kay gave up his hold on the cape and fell back a step in utter dismay.

For the mask, coming off, had brought the peaked hood with it. And there were the dancing dark curls and the merry brown eyes, and the rosy cheeks of—Rosemarie!

And she was laughing. Indeed she was laughing so hard that her knees gave out and she sank to the ground, shaking with mirth.

"Oh, I wouldn't have tripped if I hadn't got to laughing," she said, when she could stop a little. "Didn't I fool you! Oh, wasn't it fun! You never guessed it was I, all the time! How you can run, though!"

But Kay had nothing to say. He could only stare and stare. He had never been so near to Rosemarie before, or dreamed anybody could be so pretty.

At last he found his voice, and asked, "Was it always you—all the time?" He could hardly believe it.

"Yes, of course. Didn't you guess?"

"But how did you come by the mask at all?"

"Oh, one day when I was wondering what I should do, alone, and wanting, oh, so, to play with you and your sister—but old Prinie, that's my governess, said I never could—I just found it. It was blowing about the hedge. Old Prinie's nose was buried in a book and she never saw! So I hid it under my cape.

"I tried it on that night, when she left me alone to do my lessons. It was so funny! I laughed and laughed at myself in the mirror on my door. Then I got this blue cape out of Prinie's closet. It's her best Sunday cape, you must know! But I had to be covered up, didn't I! If my dress showed everybody would guess. There is a secret door—"

"Yes, behind the syringa," interrupted Kay.

Rosemarie looked at him, surprised. "Why, that's *my* secret door! What do you know about it?"

"I'll tell you afterwards. Only go on with your story."

"I found it for myself one day. I was playing Indians, you see. Since I was playing alone, I had to be all the Indians and the white settlers too. Well, the Indian chief was just about to catch a white man—only the white man tumbled back into some bushes, and then ran away and got safe. When I tumbled back among the bushes—it was the syringa bush, you know—why, I tumbled right into that door. And so I found out about it.

"I used it for all my play after that. It fitted into so many stories. It is such fun!"

"Yes, it must be. I wish we had a secret door!"

"If only Prinie would let us play together we could share it. You wouldn't need one of your own." Rosemarie spoke wistfully.

"That's why nobody thought you might be the Masker. You used the secret door." Kay was troubled now.

"Yes. Of course I use it. And then I run from tree to tree, just like the Indians, you know. Nobody has ever seen me from the windows. Prinie wouldn't be looking out anyway— not then—for she's having supper with the housekeeper. They're having it early tonight because Grandfather's coming home, and they must get me dressed for him."

"But weren't you afraid of the Policeman?"

"No. Why should I be afraid of the Policeman?"

"Didn't you know he is on the watch for you, to catch you?"

"No. Why?"

"Haven't you heard how frightened everybody is of the mask? Even some of the grown-ups! Your grandfather has told the Policeman to catch you. Not you, of course—the Masker."

"No. I didn't know all that. I wouldn't hear any of it, of course. They would think I might be frightened of the Masker myself, I suppose!" Rosemarie burst into laughter again at that quaint thought. "Oh, it would have been all the more fun if I had known that!" she laughed.

"You wouldn't have been afraid of the Policeman, if you had known?" Kay asked, wondering at her.

"Yes, perhaps, a little. But I would have gone out just the same. Oh, Kay, you must never tell on me. It will be so exciting now!"

"But I want the mask, Rosemarie. You see—" and then Kay told her all about the Wind Boy. She listened, enchanted. But when he was done, she asked, "Aren't you making it all up out of your head?"

"No, no. It is as true as true. He is very unhappy. But once he gets the mask back and has torn it up, everything will come right with him again."

"Well, of course you must take it to him then. He must be clever, the Wind Boy, to have made it so frightening. Only now, Kay, when I give it to you, how am I ever to get into your garden again, and look in at your window? If I couldn't play with you, it's been fun to frighten you and have you chase me. Why, last night, when you were after me, and I got in at my secret door–it was the most fun I have ever had in all my whole life!"

"Oh, Rosemarie, why don't you ask your grandfather. He might—"

Rosemarie shook her head. "No, he mightn't. Miss Prine is to say about everything. When she says 'No,' I must never, never ask him."

"But I should think—"

Kay had not time to say what he should think, for suddenly a voice came calling. "Rosemarie, Rose*marie!* Where are you?"

The voice sounded vexed, and frightened at the same time. For the Artist had returned a little earlier than they had expected, and Rosemarie was not to be found. Miss Prine and Polly had searched the whole house, and now they were calling in the grounds. It was Miss Prine's voice the children were hearing. She had come, in her hunting, almost to the foot of the stone steps.

"Oh, there she is!" whispered Rosemarie. "Oh bother! Stay here and hide, Kay. Here, here is the mask. Give it to the Wind Boy. Won't she just be furious about the cape, though! I don't care! It's been worth it, playing with you!"

Then she stood up and ran down the steps. Kay stayed where he was, the mask at his back.

"Oh, there you are!" he heard Miss Prine's exasperated voice exclaiming. "*In my best cape!* What will you dare next! I shall tell your grandfather."

For a long way, as they went down the grassy path, Kay heard Miss Prine's quick, scolding words.

But for some time after the voice had faded out, Kay stayed, thinking. He thought, "Rosemarie's not really naughty! It's just that she has nothing else to do but naughtiness. Nobody to play with. If she could play with Gentian and me, she wouldn't want to take Miss Prine's best cape, and not get her lessons, and frighten little children. We'd find plenty to do without that. How jolly it might be! We'd play Indians and shipwreck and everything. Gentian just wants to play fairy stories all the time. But Rosemarie's different. And there's the secret door—and all the gardens!"

He sat on, his eyes bright, thinking up the things they might do with Rosemarie. Why, there would be no end to them!

But after some time he remembered the Wind Boy and Gentian who must have come back to the goal long ago and now must be hunting for him.

He picked up the mask and ran away down the steps.

Chapter 14

Nan and the Policeman

A ND as he ran, he noticed the trodden-down flower
beds, the broken ferns, the footprints in newly
planted earth! He had done that, chasing Rosemarie. She
had done it too, of course. But then if he hadn't chased her,
she would never have gone that way! What would the
Artist say when he saw the ruin? What would Detra say
when she knew? But he had been chasing the Masker. They
couldn't blame him too much. The Masker, though, had
been Rosemarie. They could blame *her*. He was not running
now, but walking very slowly, thinking.

"I'll not tell who the Masker was," he said to himself.
"Poor Rosemarie's not to be scolded. No one needs to
know anything about it, anyway! Except the Wind Boy and
Gentian."

He started to run again, for now he could hardly wait to
get to the Wind Boy and Gentian and wave the mask in
their faces.

But I must tell you about the Wind Boy and Gentian

now. The Wind Boy had found Gentian quickly enough, and got her goal too, for her feet, even in their sandals, were no match for his strong wings. Together, then, they had hunted for Kay. Of course, they could not find him; for it never entered their heads that he might have disobeyed Detra and gone into the Artist's grounds.

For a while the Policeman, who had been there for some time, standing near the little swinging gate, kept his silence and watched Gentian searching. Of course he did not see her comrade, the Wind Boy.

After a time he called, "What are you looking for, little girl?"

"Why, we're playing hide-and-seek, and my brother has hidden himself so well we can't find him." Gentian had stopped her search to answer politely. "But if you know where he's hiding," she added quickly, "don't tell, please. It wouldn't be fair."

"That so, little girl? Well, I don't know where he ran off to, but I'm staying right here watching for him to come back, I am. If he doesn't come soon, I'll join in your game myself, and go look. He's up to some sort of mischief."

The Policeman, you must know, had watched Kay steal on his tiptoes to the hedge, crawl in, and disappear. The hedge was so high that he had not seen the Masker slipping from tree to tree on the Artist's lawn, nor Kay finally chasing it. But while he had waited for Kay to reappear, he had been thinking. And out of his thinking had come the conviction that Kay had gone to some place where he kept the mask hidden, and at twilight would come sneaking back through the hole in the hedge wearing it. For in spite of Nan, he could not give up the feeling he had had for days that this little foreign boy and nobody else was the Masker!

"Oh dear!" Gentian said so softly to the Wind Boy that the Policeman could not hear. "If he's going to stand there watching us so suspiciously, it's no fun playing any longer!"

The Wind Boy agreed. "Besides," he said, "it's deep twilight now, and time for the Masker."

"Let's sit here by the hole, not say anything, and start watching for him," Gentian suggested.

"Yes, let's," said the Wind Boy.

So they sat down on the grass, close up against the hedge, their arms wrapped about their knees, to wait and watch in the twilight. Gentian's eyes were dark with excitement. She felt sure that they must catch the Masker this time. When it came creeping through the hole, Gentian would hold it, while the Wind Boy tore off its mask. Oh, if Kay were only here to help and have the fun too! He must see it was twilight, himself. Why did he go on hiding?

The Policeman had opened the gate, and was coming in. Oh dear! What did he want now! Why couldn't he keep away till this was over! Gentian was not really afraid of the Policeman. Mother and Nan were near by, in the house, so there was nothing to be frightened of. But he was making himself a dreadful nuisance!

He came across the grass to Gentian and the Wind Boy.

"You've chosen a good place to watch," he said. "Guess I'll join you."

Gentian did not answer. She forgot politeness and stared straight ahead. Well, of course if the Policeman stayed here, and the Masker did come through the hedge, he would be the one to catch it. He was so big and strong and his arms were so long! Perhaps he'd put the mask away in his pocket when he got it, and then the Wind Boy couldn't tear it up at all, and would be as badly off as ever!

The Wind Boy had the same thoughts. He looked at Gentian with troubled, clouded eyes. "Oh bother!" he said. "Why couldn't he leave it to us?"

Gentian looked up at the Policeman. "Perhaps it won't come this twilight," she suggested. She had thought all along it was the Masker he was waiting for—and what he had said about Kay was merely teasing.

"Perhaps it will, though," the Policeman answered, looking down at her suspiciously. "Anyhow, here I sit for a while to see."

And down he did sit between Gentian and the Wind Boy! If the Wind Boy had not moved quickly the Policeman would have sat *on* him, for to the Policeman, the Wind Boy was nothing at all!

At that minute they heard running feet coming toward the hedge from the other side. It was very exciting. It must be the Masker. They were almost certain of it.

And then Kay came bounding through the hole, swinging the mask high above his head, his face shining.

The Policeman sprang and grabbed him by the shoulder.

"There now! I was right. I shouldn't have listened to that girl Nan!"

Kay was taken by surprise, of course, but he was not frightened—only startled. When he saw Gentian and the Wind Boy, he smiled as though a policeman having him by the shoulder and frowning like a thundercloud was nothing. But the Policeman mustn't get his hands on the mask!

"For you, Wind Boy," Kay cried, and tried to toss the mask over the Policeman's head to him.

But the Policeman was too quick for him, and got it. "That there mask goes with me. It's my proof that I caught the Masker," he shouted.

He held it fast in his muscular hand.

"*You* caught the Masker!" Kay cried. "How can you say such a thing? You weren't even there."

"Well, I always guessed that you were the Masker, you young rascal. But now I've caught you red-handed, with the thing itself!"

"No, no!" Kay protested. "I chased the Masker and caught her—it. I took the mask and came running with it to the Wind Boy. It's really his, you know, since he made it."

The Policeman paid no attention to the mention of the Wind Boy.

"Well, son," he asked, "who was the Masker then, if 'twasn't yourself? Out with it!"

But Kay's sure smile had frozen and died. He answered only with silence.

At his silence, Gentian and the Wind Boy were amazed. But the Policeman grinned.

"Oh, do tell us quickly, Kay," Gentian pleaded. "He mustn't think *you're* the Masker."

But Kay stared straight before him. "I'm not going to tell," he said quietly. "It ought to be enough that I've got the mask and it won't frighten children ever again."

"Oh, it was you all right," the Policeman said, delighted with his own cleverness. "And you had everyone but me well fooled. Even that Nan there, who's smart enough to have known better."

"Oh, Kay," Gentian was almost crying, "how can you let him say that?"

Nan, from a window in the little brown house, had seen

the Policeman out there in the twilight, the mask in one hand, the other gripping Kay's shoulder. She came running.

"What is it?" she asked the Policeman. "You've got the mask! Good! But why are you holding Kay so?"

"I'm holding him so because he's a mischievous scamp, and you should have known it! Now I'm going to march him in to his mother, and inform her. Then to the Artist, for the reward. He's just come home. Between the two, what's to be done with the boy will be decided."

But Nan laughed. And the children looked at her in grieved surprise. How could she laugh, and they in such trouble!

She said, "I know very well, Officer, that the Masker was never Kay. Why, just last evening, when Kay and Gentian were sitting at the supper table, the Masker looked in at the window! Now he couldn't be in two places at once, could he—at the table and at the window?"

"And, Nan," Kay put in, glad of this sensible ally, "it was I myself who chased the Masker tonight, and got the mask away from her—*it*. I was just bringing it to the Wind Boy, when the Policeman grabbed me."

"That's all very fine sounding," said the Policeman, "but he can't tell us who the Masker was, or what!"

"It's not that I can't. I won't."

"Let me see the horrid thing," Nan commanded—but gently, holding out her hand for it.

"Be careful, then," the Policeman cautioned her. "Nothing must happen to it till the Artist has had a look. He never *would* believe it was as horrible as I said. He always laughed at me."

Nan held the mask up and looked it square in its green eyes.

"You are rather horrible, but you are funny, too!" She spoke to it as though it were alive and could hear. "It was only mischief that made you first, but then you grew into something worse. You frightened little children. You made one little boy sick. That was wicked of you. So now you must be torn to bits and thrown away on the wind, and never, never, never frighten children again."

The Policeman was startled by Nan's last words. He stepped quickly toward her to take back the mask. But Nan was too quick for him. She whirled about and tossed it to the Wind Boy.

He caught it with glad eagerness and rushed away, tearing it to little bits as he went. The brown and green leaves and twigs that made it were scattered all about on the grass. Gentian and Kay saw the Wind Boy lift his wings then and fly away, up into the twilight air. For a minute there was the other village hanging above their own—other houses, other gardens, and away off the other woods and other mountains, all clear in crystal twilight.

But quickly the Policeman's voice called them back, and they forgot the Clear Land.

"Now you've done it!" he cried to Nan. "You might have seen how easy broke it was! What did you mean by tossing it up like that?"

For all that the Policeman had seen—too bad for him!—was Nan throwing the mask into the air, and then it being whirled about in a sudden burst of spring wind, and scattered in tiny pieces over the grass.

But Nan did not look a bit sorry. And neither did she seem afraid of the Policeman.

No. She went directly to him and lightly lifted his hand from Kay's shoulder. "He'll not run away from you," she said. "Don't you see that he's only a little boy and has no place to run to, except his mother back there in the house?"

"Well, I suppose you're right. He couldn't escape us, now he's found out. We'd best march him to his mother. Come along, young man."

But Nan stood in front of him. "Please don't tell his mother tonight," she said. "She has only just this minute started to work on a little statue she is making. Evening is her only time for this work she loves best, for all day she has to be at the factory. If you go in and disturb her now, she may not be able to get back to work tonight at all. Artists are like that."

The Policeman stared. "So? But she's got to know. Something's got to be done to him. When may I tell her?"

"Tomorrow evening when she comes from the factory. Then you may tell her. Until then I promise you Kay will not run away."

"All right. I hadn't the mind to disturb her the other night either. Remember? When you live in a town with a great Artist," he nodded his head toward the Artist's mansion, over the hedge, "you get to know something about artists, and the way they work! But I'll go along to *him* now. He does *his* work mornings."

"Yes, do go to the Artist. I'm sure he won't mind your not having the mask to show. You can say it was my fault, its getting broken."

But the Policeman made no move to go for a minute. He was looking into Nan's eyes again. Or rather, he was looking through them to the purple mountains, with calm stars just risen in the sky above.

"No, I'd not tell on you, not for the world," he said. "You can rest easy about that. But it was careless!"

Then he went.

Nan turned to Kay. "Oh, I didn't! I didn't!" he assured her. "I never was the Masker!"

"Don't I know it?" Nan hushed him, putting an arm across his shoulder.

"But you told him to tell Mother tomorrow!"

"Why, Kay," Gentian said, "Mother will believe you. You have only to tell her it wasn't you."

Kay straightened. "Of course, she won't punish me when I say it wasn't I. It isn't that that bothers me. It's how she'll *feel*. She wants people to like us. And now they'll all think us queerer than ever. Not only queer–bad! Perhaps I'll be expelled from school. And Mother will be miserable. And it will all be my fault!"

"Well, anyway, let's be glad that she's not to be troubled tonight," Nan said. "For, now that the Wind Boy is happy again, and back with his comrades, this is her chance to get the statuette right. He will look glad of his wings tomorrow, and have clear eyes."

"Oh, do you think the Wind Boy will come back tonight so that she can see how happy he is?"

"Hardly so soon, when he has just got his comrades back. But your mother may follow him to the Clear Land. That is where she does her true work, you know, even if she does forget about it when she's back."

With an arm across each child's shoulder Nan turned to the house.

"Let's steal in very softly and up to my room," she whispered, when they had come to the door. "Your mother must not be called back from the Clear Land until she has got the Wind Boy just as he is now into her plastilina. That would spoil everything."

But as they slipped past the sitting room's open door, they looked in at Detra. The statuette was before her on the table, and her fingers were working quickly and surely on the brow. Her eyes looked straight at Kay, but without seeing. For this was not the real Detra here, their own mother. *She* was off in the Clear Land watching the Wind Boy at play with his comrades. This that the children saw was only her *mechanical* self—you know, the self that walks and runs and leads you about if you ever chance to walk in your sleep. That self, that part of you, never can go up into the Clear Land.

The children made no noise on the stairs. But when

Nan's door was closed behind them, then they could speak. But even then they were careful and kept their voices hushed. No sound must drift down from the window and into the room where Detra was working on the Wind Boy.

Nan told them stories. Gentian sat at her feet leaning against her knee, but Kay sprawled on the floor, his chin in his hands, his eyes looking out into the darkening night. And though Nan's stories were wonderful and magical, still Kay heard little of them that night; for he was promising himself over and over, "I won't tell on Rosemarie. No, no matter what they do. I'll not tell even Mother. A good thing the Policeman didn't guess! I'm glad, glad he didn't guess!"

But, even so, he dreaded tomorrow.

Chapter 15

Rosemarie Is Waked by the Little Silver Bell

As for Rosemarie, Miss Prine scolded her all the way back to the house. She scolded her for leaving her lessons to run out to play. She scolded her for going out into the twilight alone and without permission. She scolded her for "stealing" and abusing Miss Prine's own best cape. But most of all she scolded her for not being sorry. For Rosemarie refused to be sorry. She did not drop her head, and whenever Miss Prine turned to look down into her face, she saw a happiness there that there was no accounting for—and that was indeed offensive under the circumstances.

Of course the thing that was keeping Rosemarie happy, in spite of the disgrace that was her due, was the memory of Kay. Why, for half an hour or so she had had a real play-mate! When he chased her in the mask—that had been a sort of game of tag, hadn't it? Rosemarie had seen other children playing tag before, but *she* had never played it—for you can't play tag alone! And then they had talked in the tulip garden, and he had told her all that fairy-storyish thing about the Wind Boy! Only it wasn't a fairy story. He had said it was true, and he looked true enough when he said it all. *She* had only met fairies in books! But those two, Kay and Gentian, knew them in real life and had them for friends. When they had each other, was it fair that they should have the fairies too?

Miss Prine's voice was getting lower and lower in its scolding tones the nearer they came to the house, for—in spite of what she'd said about telling him—she did not mean the Artist to know how very naughty Rosemarie had been. He might think it was in some way *her* fault—that she had not kept careful enough watch. And that would be unjust, for no one could be more watchful than Miss Prine. It was just that she had been eating her supper with the housekeeper, and thought Rosemarie would be safe with her lesson books.

So very quietly now, she hurried Rosemarie up the back stairs to her high nursery. There she brushed and brushed her dark, dancing curls with quick firm strokes until they stopped dancing and shone instead. Then, very hurriedly, she slipped her into a fresh frock. This should have been Polly's work, but Polly was still hunting somewhere in the grounds. There had not been time to tell her that Rosemarie was found.

Now Rosemarie stood prim and sweet and clean, ready to be seen by her grandfather. And they were only just in

time, for there was his knock at the door. He had unexpect-
edly come up to the nursery instead of waiting for her to be
brought down.

Rosemarie was glad to see her grandfather, for she loved
him with her whole heart. At least it had been her whole
heart until Kay and Gentian had moved in next door, and
from a distance she had begun loving them too. But she
was a little in awe of him, for all her love. And then Miss
Prine always appeared a little afraid of him. That had had its
effect on Rosemarie from her babyhood!

His first words tonight amazed her. "Well, have you
been having a good time with that little girl and boy next
door? Better than playing always alone, eh?"

But Miss Prine interrupted quickly and nervously, before Rosemarie could answer.

"Oh, we haven't begun that yet," she said. "You did not
say there was any hurry about it in your telegram. And right
on top of your telegram came the news from the Policeman
that both those foreign children were mischievous beyond
the ordinary, and that he suspected the boy of being the
Masker. So—"

But at the word "Masker" the Artist had sternly mo-
tioned Miss Prine silent.

"We will not discuss this before Rosemarie, if you
please."

"Sir, I am sorry for the slip," Miss Prine went out of the
room, leaving Rosemarie alone with her grandfather.

"Oh, Grandfather, did you tell her I might play with

them?" Rosemarie asked with clasped hands and delight in her face.

"Yes, I did wire something of the sort to Miss Prine. But I shall have to have a talk with her now before it is definitely decided. We will say no more until that time. Only tell me what you have been doing while I was away."

Rosemarie was surprised at this request. Usually her famous grandfather was too absorbed in his work and his books and his clever friends to give thought to her adventures. But Miss Prine had trained her so well that she was ready for the social emergency. She sat down on a footstool at her grandfather's knee, and told him her days. That is, she told him of everything but the masquerading. She dared not, of course, tell him that!

But he scarcely heard her words. He was looking at her in a musing, troubled fashion. You see, he had been thinking of Gentian in the time he was away, and of what she had said of Rosemarie. It was Gentian who had set him to thinking.

Right in the middle of the account of Rosemarie's lonely adventures, came a knock at the door, and there was Miss Prine again.

"The village Policeman is down in the hall again. It's the third time this evening. Shall we say you're still busy?"

"No—no. I'll come. And we will finish this tomorrow," the Artist promised Rosemarie. "It is bedtime now, anyway. Good night, and sleep well."

But out in the passage he asked of Miss Prine in a low

voice, quickly, "Tell me: You spoke of the Masker before the child! Has she been allowed to hear anything about it? That was against my strictest orders. Has she been frightened?"

"No indeed. She has heard nothing," Miss Prine assured him. "It was just in my eagerness not to let you think that I had acted inadvisedly in not allowing her to play with those dreadful children that I let the word slip. Aside from this single time, she has heard not a word."

"Why do you call them 'dreadful children'? I liked the little girl ever so much. I had quite a talk with her in the tulip garden."

"Yes, I dare say you would notice nothing. They are quiet enough, and well-spoken. Clean too. But the Policeman has a tale for you about them that may make you change your mind as to letting Rosemarie have them for playmates."

"Is that what the Policeman wants now, to complain about those youngsters?"

"Yes, he caught the boy with the mask. He's come about that."

The Artist's face grew more and more sober all the way down the stairs, as he thought about this.

You know all that the Policeman had to tell him, and so you shall hear what happened to Rosemarie that night. For a wonderful thing did happen.

She went to bed with a glad heart. For had not her grandfather hinted that she might be allowed to play with Kay and Gentian?

Oh, if only she were let do that she would try never to

be naughty again! She wondered if Kay had got the mask safely to the Wind Boy, and was the Wind Boy back with his comrades now, one of them again, in the Clear Land? Perhaps she herself would see the Wind Boy some time. Kay had said that he liked to take his naps in the tulip garden. Tomorrow she would go softly there, and watch. She would make Miss Prine sit on the lowest stone step and wait for her; for Rosemarie was not supposed to go so far as the tulip garden by herself. Yes, she would surely look for the Wind Boy in the tulip garden tomorrow.

In the midst of these happy thoughts she fell asleep.

On a stand at the head of Rosemarie's bed stood a little silver bell. This was for her to ring if she should wake in the night and want anything. She never did ring it, for she always slept right through the night as healthy children should.

But tonight a strange thing happened. The little silver bell at the head of her bed was rung, ever so lightly, but not by Rosemarie. It was rung so softly that Miss Prine, sleeping in the next room with the door ajar, did not hear it at all. But being right at Rosemarie's ear, it woke her.

She sat up in her bed. Who had rung it? The room was silvery with starlight and Rosemarie could see about in it quite well. Over by one of the windows, the window where the big doll house stood, was something brighter than the starlight. When Rosemarie looked at it hard, she saw that it was a person.

"Who *are* you?" she whispered through the room, for

she was not sure at first that it was not just a dream she was having.

The person did not answer at once, but moved toward her in starry-brightness. She came to the edge of Rosemarie's bed, and sat down there, on the silk coverlet.

"Don't you know who I am?" the starry person asked then.

"Why, you're Nan, the maid next door."

"Yes, I am Nan."

"But what a beautiful robe you are wearing! It's like the sky. It makes you like a fairy. No, nicer than any fairy!"

"Do you like it so much? Gentian does too. And now she has made herself one like it."

"Gentian has! Oh, if I am allowed to play with her, will she let me see it? Is it really as beautiful as yours? I thought she had only shabby, faded clothes, rather funny ones. Will she show me her starry one?"

"Yes, I think she would, if you *were* allowed to play with her. But now you will not be allowed, for your grandfather will think it dangerous."

"Oh, but he has promised that perhaps I may. Only tonight! Truly."

"That was before he saw the Policeman."

They were whispering, their faces close. Nan's eyes were more sky-like than her nightgown, and her face was shining too. There was a smell of pine needles about her and spruce, green leaves, and arbutus blossoms.

Rosemarie's breath was stopped with wonder. "You

smell like the woods," she said, forgetting Nan's words of the Policeman and what they might mean.

"I have just come from the mountains."

"Not just tonight? How could you get 'way there and back just tonight? I saw you from my window at supper time!"

"Oh, in my starry-brightness—that's what Gentian calls this nightgown—I can do that easily enough."

Rosemarie reached her hand to touch the starry stuff. But her fingers felt nothing at all! She might as well have tried to touch starlight.

"Are you a dream?" she whispered. "Am I asleep?"

Nan laughed merrily at that. Strange that that laugh did not waken Miss Prine!

"Not at all, Rosemarie! Could a dream ring your bell, do you think?"

"You *did* ring my bell, didn't you! That was what woke me. But if you *did* ring it, then how did you get way over to the window there before I could open my eyes?"

Nan laughed again, and still Miss Prine didn't wake. "If you will promise not to think me a dream, I will tell you," she said, leaning close, until Rosemarie saw deep into her eyes. "Well, then, I rang the bell while I was still in the mountains. Can you believe that? I came all the way in the instant while you were waking, after I had rung the bell!"

Rosemarie gasped. "Truly? Truly?" she asked.

But really she did not mean to ask, for she knew very well that it was truly, truly. It was only her surprise.

But to come all the way from the mountains in the instant waking took! It was too strange to understand, but never too strange to believe, when Nan said it.

"Why can't I touch you, since you're real and not a dream?" Rosemarie asked.

"Because I'm in my starry-brightness."

"Oh, is your nightrobe *magic?*"

"No, of course not. Miss Prine wouldn't want you to be so superstitious!" Nan was still laughing.

"But what else but magic can keep me from touching you, and let you travel so fast, and ring a bell from all that way away?"

"Dear Rosemarie, if I could tell you that, I would be very wonderful. I myself don't know the 'hows' of it. I'm just a girl from the mountains."

They were silent for a while, while Rosemarie wondered. But she kept her gaze on Nan's eyes of sky and knew it was no dream. Then she remembered what Nan had said of the Policeman.

"What about the Policeman? How can *he* stop me from playing with Gentian and Kay?" she asked.

"Well, you see he came tonight to tell your grandfather that Kay is the Masker. Your grandfather won't like that. He'll think Kay's not a child you should play with."

"But Kay isn't the Masker. So grandfather can't—"

Nan didn't say anything; she merely looked at Rosemarie.

"But if I tell him *I'm* the Masker what will they do to me? What will the Policeman do?"

"I don't know. But I do know, for the Policeman has told me, what will happen to Kay, unless you tell. He'll be expelled from school for a week. And his mother will be very sad."

"Oh bother! But why doesn't Kay tell them himself? He will, won't he?"

"Oh, no. He didn't even tell *me* you're the Masker."

"How did you know then?"

"I guessed."

"Oh dear! What shall I do? Why *won't* Kay tell?"

"He doesn't want you to be scolded. He must be fond of you."

"What can I do?"

"What do you think you can do?"

There was a silence. Then Rosemarie said, "But I am afraid of Grandfather! More afraid of him, really, than of the Policeman!"

Nan said nothing.

"Well, must I tell him?"

Nan did not answer that either.

"And when I do, I suppose I'll never be allowed to play with Kay and Gentian ever. That would be the biggest punishment he could make! I didn't know I was being so naughty, truly. I didn't know about the little boy who was made sick until Kay told me. It was only a game."

"Yes, I know."

With Nan's eyes of sky so close to hers, Rosemarie suddenly had to stop feeling sorry for herself. Self-pity faded into nothingness.

"When shall I tell him?" she asked.

"Now, so that you can sleep well. He is sitting up late in his study. I saw the light as I came toward the house."

"Oh, did you come in through the secret door?" Rosemarie asked then, delighted by the sudden thought. "It is *my* secret door, you know. How did you find it?"

"Not by the secret door you mean. But it was a secret door, and I found it for myself. Indeed it was the only way I could come to you tonight."

"Wasn't it the door behind the syringa bush? That's the only secret door I know of." Rosemarie's eyes were sparkling at the mystery of it.

"No, not the door behind the syringa bush."

"Where, where is there another?" Rosemarie was all eagerness.

"My secret door was a little one I found waiting ajar—a little door in your mind."

Rosemarie shook her curls at that. It was no use trying to understand.

"I'll go to Grandfather, now," she said, putting her feet out of bed. "Do you suppose he will be terribly angry?"

"I don't know. I hope not, for I don't think that you were really very naughty."

But when Rosemarie had opened the door into the passage she looked back at Nan. "It's pitch dark," she whispered. "All the lights are out, and everyone's in bed."

It was true. The passage and the stairs were in utter darkness, except for a thin, pale starlight that came from a high window somewhere.

Rosemarie ran back to Nan. But in the middle of the room she stopped. Being a coward was no good. But she asked, "Will you be waiting here when I get back—to tuck me in, Nan?"

"Yes, I'll be waiting," Nan promised.

So Rosemarie took heart and went out into the dark hallway again. There she felt her way along the wall to the stairs. No starlight reached the stairs, and all was utter darkness. Rosemarie had her eyes tight shut all the way down. But that made no difference; she could have seen nothing with them open.

There was more starlight in the hall beneath, and that helped her to the second flight of stairs. They were long and turning. But at their foot was her grandfather's library door. Rosemarie, to her mingled relief and fear, saw the light shining through a crack at the bottom. She knocked, ever so softly.

"Who is there?"

"I. Rosemarie."

The Artist came in quick strides to the door and flung it open. He looked down in amazement at Rosemarie, in her little white nightgown and bare feet.

"Oh, Grandfather, there is something I must tell you!"

"Couldn't it wait until morning, my dear child?"

"No. At least, Nan thought I couldn't sleep well till you knew."

"Who is Nan?"

"The girl from the mountains. But it's the Masker I've got to tell you about. Oh, Grandfather, I'm the Masker! I was, all the time. Kay knew nothing about it—till tonight, when he caught me at it and made me give him the mask for the Wind Boy."

The Artist brows knit into a puzzled frown. What was all this about a girl from the mountains, and the Wind Boy! Was it Gentian's Wind Boy? And Rosemarie the Masker! And what was she doing here, his perfectly cared-for little granddaughter, standing in the dark, drafty hall in her nightgown and bare feet? Where was Miss Prine, anyway? What was it all about?

He ran his hand through his clustering gray curls—curls so like the Wind Boy's. Then he led Rosemarie into the room and made her sit on the sofa. He wrapped her round and round, bare feet and all, in a gay, striped Roman shawl, and sat beside her.

"Now, Rosemarie, begin at the very beginning, and tell me everything. Don't cry. (Rosemarie had not known there were tears in her eyes.) How could you be the Masker? That's absurd."

So Rosemarie wiped away the surprising tears with a corner of the shawl, and did tell her grandfather everything.

When she had come to an end, he sat silent for some time. But, after a while, he said, slowly, wonderingly, "Nan

in starry-brightness in your room must have been a dream.
And the Wind Boy—well perhaps he's a dream of Gentian
and Kay's. But all the rest seems real enough."

And then, to Rosemarie's utter surprise, her grandfather
suddenly took her upon his knee, Roman shawl and all,
and leaned her head against his shoulder. "How lonely you
have been!" he said in the saddest, kindest voice. "It is all
your selfish old grandfather's fault. You should have had
playmates all this while. *Mea culpa!*"

They sat that way for a long time, not saying anything.

... And after a time, Rosemarie, in spite of the deliciousness of being loved by her grandfather, fell asleep.

When she woke, it was morning, and she was back in her bed in her high nursery room. But it was still very early, and Miss Prine was not yet stirring.

Rosemarie lay, the only one awake, in the big still house. Right at once, though, she knew that last night had not been a dream, for she was still wrapped around in the Roman shawl from the sofa in her grandfather's library. Oh, wouldn't Miss Prine be surprised when she found her so! But she couldn't scold. Grandfather wouldn't let her.

Rosemarie sat up. There was sunlight instead of starlight at the windows now. But over the silk coverlet and all through the room hung, faintly, the smell of pine and spruce and green leaves and arbutus. Oh, why hadn't she kept herself awake to say "good night" to Nan!

Chapter 16

Rosemarie Comes to School

IN the little brown house over the hedge Kay was waking too. But even before his eyes were open, he remembered that something unpleasant was waiting for him in this day. What was it? Oh, yes, the mask business. The Policeman had told the Artist that he, Kay, was the Masker. Before night everyone in the village would think he was the Masker—everyone, that is, except Gentian and Nan and Detra. *They* would not believe the Policeman, but they would be bothered all the same.

But why was Gentian laughing? Had she forgotten all about last night and the Policeman?

Kay jumped out of bed and ran to the head of the stairs. The laughter was coming up from the sitting room. And Gentian only laughed like that when she was very, very happy.

"What is it? Why are you laughing?" Kay called down to her.

At his voice she came dancing out into the hall. She was

still in her nightgown, and her hair was all rumpled from her pillow. Her cheeks were rosy from sleep.

"Oh, Kay," she cried. "Do come and see the Wind Boy! He is perfect!"

"Is the Wind Boy down there? Hello, Wind Boy!" Kay sang out.

"Oh no. Not our Wind Boy. The statuette. I could hardly wait for morning to see if Mother had followed him to the Clear Land, and got him happy. I was awake before dawn."

But Kay was bounding down the stairs. He had forgotten about the statuette. Of course! Well, some good thing had come out of last night!

Detra was just finishing her early breakfast. And right in the middle of the table in front of the tulips, the early sun just touching his head, stood the finished Wind Boy.

Kay went close, and stood looking. Yes, Gentian was right. He was perfect. It was the Wind Boy as he had looked when he caught the mask that Nan had thrown, and scattered it to bits on the lawn. His face, and body too, were all alight and joyous. He was about to fly up, up and away into the blue air. He was standing on very tiptoes, his wings spread wide, his whole body–every bit of him–ready.

Indeed the statuette, little as it was, and made only of plastilina, was so alive and lightened from within it was not easy for the children to remember that it was just a statuette and not the Wind Boy himself.

"Oh, Mother! He is just himself. As he became last night! Nan was right. You did follow him up there then!"

Detra was smiling happily, but sleepily. She had not been to bed at all, but had worked all night in the Clear Land.

"Yes," she said, "last night he was different. I saw him right. He had never been like that before. There was always a cloud over him somehow. But last night he shone out to my eyes clear and radiant like this. Oh, I have never, never done work of this sort before. I know that."

Kay and Gentian were looking at each other now. Their eyes said, "She thinks *she* did it. But it was really us—ourselves and Nan. *We* made the Wind Boy happy."

And Kay exclaimed aloud, "I don't care now. They can do what they want to me. It was worth it."

Detra looked away from the statuette and at Kay, puzzled. "What don't you care about, Kay? What is worth it? And worth what?"

But with her words, the village clock began to strike. It was seven o'clock.

"Oh, I must hurry," Detra cried, jumping up, "or I shall miss my train."

She suddenly kissed and hugged both her children, snatched up her cape, and ran away out of the house.

But Kay had meant what he said. The statuette was so lovely, and his mother was made so happy by it, that he was now ready to face the day, and all the humiliation it might hold for him. When school time came he was ready for it. What did school matter, since all the really important things had got themselves so very right at last!

But the minute he got into the school yard, he knew

that the Policeman had already spread the news of having caught him with the mask. The children, playing around the door, pretended great fear and ran away shrieking.

There was nothing Kay could do but march in and take his accustomed seat, and there wait for what would come next.

Miss Todd, he thought, kept her gaze on him steadily and strangely from the very first. There was an unusual hubbub in the room, but it stopped when he entered.

Then school began.

Kay's cheeks were afire, but his head was very, very high. He was thinking: "I'm glad Mother won't know till tonight anyway. She'll have all day to think about the Wind Boy and be happy." But he was sorry for Gentian who was sitting very erect behind her little desk, with her hands tightly clasped in her lap and her lips set together.

At first school went as usual. Miss Todd's good order and drill were not to be shaken by the excitement that lay under the morning. But whenever Kay looked up from his books or paper, he seemed to find her keen eyes upon him. And she did not call on him to recite, although his turn came over and over. She passed him by, but still looking at him.

Never had school seemed so long to Kay and Gentian, though truly it had often seemed long enough!

Well, if Kay was to be expelled and put to shame, why didn't Miss Todd do it now? That would be better than this! Behind the ticking of the school clock, and the lessons and the recitations, the whole school was simply waiting for some sort of excitement. Everyone knew that. And then, toward recess time, at last it came!

A step out in the hall. A boy near Kay whispered, "The Policeman!"

So that was it! They had been waiting for the Policeman to come to take him away to prison. In his own country they did not put little boys into prison, but who knew what they might or might not do here in this strange, foreign land!

Well, let them. Now, less than ever, did he mean to tell on Rosemarie.

A knock sounded on the door.

Everyone jumped a little, even Miss Todd—just as though, after the steps, they had not been expecting a knock.

Kay straightened back his shoulders and tried not to look at Gentian. But somehow he could not help seeing her—her wide, blue gentian eyes swam before his gaze, eyes terrified for him.

Then Miss Todd opened the door. And there came in not the Policeman, but the Artist, and with him Rosemarie!

The school gasped in its surprise. You could hear it all about the room. But the Artist did not take the chair Miss Todd so politely offered him. He came and stood by her desk and looked at the children. He looked at them all in turn, and they looked back. It made Gentian think of the Shoeman who had measured her and Kay by looking into their eyes. What was the great Artist measuring them for?

When he came to Gentian he smiled a greeting. But she could not smile back. She was too frightened for Kay.

But the Artist seemed to understand her soberness.

He spoke rather quickly then, in a low, clear voice.

"I have come to tell you that the Masker has been found," he said, "and that it will not frighten you again at twilight. You can play on the streets near my house now without thought of it. It will never come again."

Miss Todd at her desk nodded. And now there was no doubt about it any longer—she was looking at Kay in great sternness. But the Artist was not stern. He said, "And the Policeman assures me that he knows who the Masker was.

It was, he says a boy—a boy in this school. Indeed, he caught him with the mask in his hands. His name is Kay. Is Kay here now?"

"Kay, stand up." Miss Todd's voice, to Kay's surprise, had sorriness mixed with its sternness.

Kay stood up by his seat.

The Artist looked at him kindly. But Kay was too miserable to see that.

"I hear that for many days, always at twilight, Kay, you have gone around in a horrid mask, frightening other children. The Policeman caught you with the mask, so he thinks it must have been you all the time. Was it?"

"He did catch me with the mask. But I never wore it, or frightened anyone with it."

"Then who did?"

Kay did not answer that. He stayed silent, trying hard not to look at Rosemarie.

"Won't you tell?"

"No, sir, I won't."

All the other children and even Miss Todd gasped at Kay's coolness.

It must have been because Kay was a foreigner and did not know how great a man the Artist was, and how important to this village, that he dared speak so firmly his "No!" Why, the Artist had given them this very school, and its big playground. No other village of its size in the country had such a fine school and playground.

But the Artist did not mind Kay's seeming fearlessness.

He said: "Well, Kay, if you won't tell, Rosemarie will. Rosemarie is here just for that." He turned and looked down at his little granddaughter.

Rosemarie had stood all this while looking at no one in the school but Kay. She was a little shy at being up there before all the eyes of the village children, but aside from that shyness she was her natural self, her merry self, with dimples just around the corner.

Now that her grandfather had turned to her she had to speak. She did it quickly, rather breathlessly, and still looking at Kay.

"*I* was the Masker. It was I who frightened you all. My governess has her supper at twilight, and then I could get out without her knowing. Last night Kay chased me and caught me, and I gave him the mask. He was taking it back to the Wind Boy to tear up, when the Policeman caught him. He never wore it at all."

Never was a schoolroom more silent than that school was for a minute after Rosemarie had finished—till the Artist spoke again.

"Rosemarie didn't know about the little boy who was made sick. You see, we did not want *her* to be frightened, and so no one mentioned the Masker to her ever, or what harm it was doing. Rosemarie had no children to play with. And so she found that running around in the twilight, frightening people and looking in at windows where there were children, was the next best thing to having playmates.

"That is why it would not be fair to punish her for her

masquerading—any more than she has already been punished. And now I want her to have children to play with
forever after, so that she will not have to look into windows.
And so I am here to ask Miss Todd if she may come to this
school, and indeed begin working with you and playing
with you this very morning!"

And then the Artist added one thing more. "I hope you
will all be friends with Rosemarie, for she needs your friendship. But you know, from what has happened, that she has
one true and loyal friend here already—and that is Kay."

Then, after a few quiet words at the door with Miss Todd,
the Artist went away, leaving Rosemarie at school. Just at first
the children could hardly attend to their lessons. Before this
they had only glimpsed Rosemarie in the distance. She
seemed like a child in a moving picture more than in real life.
And now here she was, one of them, in a plain gingham
frock and with everyday leather sandals and brown socks.
Why, she looked just like any other of the little girls!

But almost at once Rosemarie's merry brown eyes and
the toss of her dark dancing curls did away with their feelings
of shyness. Even before recess came and they ran out to play,
they had discovered that she was a regular, real little girl.

But recess did add the finishing touch. Rosemarie was
such fun! You would think she had been playing with other
children all her life. Perhaps that was because she had so often *imagined* what she would do, had she children to play
with.

And of course, Rosemarie never, as the other children

had done in the past, left Gentian and Kay out. Rather, they were the first she turned to in everything. Had she not been watching them from her high nursery window for months now? Did she not know them well? Better even than their schoolmates knew them?

So, for the first time since they had come to this village, Kay and Gentian forgot that they were foreigners and left off all strangeness. They raced and shouted and laughed with the rest.

And at the close of school Rosemarie ran home between them, the happiest little girl in the village.

But she pulled them to a stop at a corner. "How *can* you run so fast?" she asked. "My breath's gone."

"It's the sandals, I think," Kay answered.

And then all the rest of the way home they walked very slowly, for Kay and Gentian had to tell Rosemarie about the Shoeman and his blue-curtained store with the crystal light flooding down the stairs, and the little ovenbird in place of a doorbell. Rosemarie believed it all and loved it.

Gentian and Kay were very late in getting home from school that day.

When Nan saw their faces, she asked, "What happened to you? Was school so wonderful?"

"Oh, it was!" they cried. And then, between them, they told her all about the morning. Nan was as happy as they over all that had happened.

"And from now on school will never seem unpleasant to you again," she said when they were done. "You will go

there gladly every morning, just as the other children do. It
is your school now, and the village will get to be your
village. That is just as your mother wants it. How glad she
will be!"

But they were hardly done with their dinner, because
they had talked so much, before Rosemarie came skipping
through the hole in the hedge just as though she had been
doing it always, and was at their window.

Her dancing curls and merry eyes might have belonged
to some fairy, but her cheeks were too hard and rosy for any
but a very human little girl!

"Come in! Come in!" cried the children.

"No. Come out!" called back Rosemarie. "Let's play in
the tulip garden. Grandfather says we may and without
Miss Prine's coming along to bother! Think of that!"

"But Mother doesn't let us go there," the children said
wistfully.

Nan had heard from the kitchen, and came quickly into
the sitting room. "Your mother would not mind your going
through the hedge now," she assured them, "since it's Rosemarie herself that asked you. It was only because she
thought you were not wanted there that she forbade it before."

Rosemarie had run around and in at the door, and was in
the room with them. To Gentian's and Kay's surprise, she
threw her arms about Nan's neck and gave her a great hug.

"Do you know Nan?" they asked.

"Of course I do. Didn't she come in starry-brightness to

tell me everything and make me brave? Grandfather thinks
she was only a dream. But he won't think so when we show
her to him! And see what she made happen! I'm your playmate now. I'm even going to your school! A funny dream
to manage all that!"

Then Nan and Gentian and Kay and Rosemarie all
laughed together—though Kay and Gentian did not yet
know exactly what it was about. And just as Gentian, Monday morning up in the Clear School, had danced 'round
and 'round in the arbor and then out of it—so here now
these four took hands and danced 'round and 'round in the

room and out the door, and there 'round and 'round under the cherry tree, to the music of their laughter.

It was Nan who stopped first. "I am forgetting all about the dishes," she said.

At that they laughed more. "What a thing to remember!" Rosemarie cried.

But Kay said, "Nan is like that. If there weren't dishes, or some such thing to be done, I think she'd fly straight away and be a fairy."

"May we help you with the dishes then?" asked Rosemarie. "I never was let help with any housework, no matter how much I teased to!"

So the children went in with Nan and helped clear the table. Nan gave them a clean towel each—a towel with the sunshine still in it, for they had come from the line at the door where Nan had hung them that morning—and after she had dipped the glasses and plates, knives and forks into rainbow soap suds and washed them well, the children took them to dry.

Then Rosemarie, because she was so eager to be in on everything, was allowed to sweep up the crumbs under the table, while Kay held the dustpan for her, and to hang the newly washed towels out in the sunshine at the back door again.

"Now for the tulip garden," Kay cried, who had grown a little impatient of all this housework.

"Good-by, then. Come home in time for supper," Nan said.

"Oh, but you come too, Nan," Rosemarie pleaded. "It will be so much more fun with you along!"

"But I thought you didn't want a grown-up. Miss Prine's not going."

Rosemarie laughed.

"Well, you're not Miss Prine," she said. "Why, you're like us. *Only more so!*"

So Nan put off the mending she had intended to do until evening, and ran way with the children through the hole in the hedge, and down the grassy paths toward the tulip garden.

Chapter 17

Detra Meets the Artist

WHEN they got there it was Nan who thought up the most wonderful things to play. They were games the children had never heard of before, and they were the greatest fun. Afterwards they could never play them over again, for somehow they could not remember how they had gone. That was strange, for at the time they had not seemed complicated, but simple as day. They found themselves in these games jumping farther than they had known they could jump, climbing higher, and hiding in more secret and smaller places than they would have dreamed themselves able to before.

But after a while they grew tired of even these wonderful games, and threw themselves down in the grassy center of the tulip garden to rest.

"Now," said Rosemarie, "tell me more about the Wind Boy."

"But we have told you all," Kay answered. "There is nothing more."

"Well, if he's real, and not just a pretend game of yours," Rosemarie asked, teasingly, "why doesn't he come and play with us now?"

"Why? I don't know. Perhaps he will. Perhaps he's been around all this time wanting to play with us."

But Gentian shook her head. "No, Kay. He's nowhere about. I've been watching for him all afternoon. I would have seen him if he was anywhere around."

"Now that he has his Clear Children playmates back, perhaps he won't want to come down here anymore. Perhaps he only came before because he was lonely," Kay said.

Gentian did not answer that. She herself had been thinking exactly that thing for hours, with this difference—that she had not the heart to speak it.

"Let's try to see up into the Clear Land," Rosemarie suggested then. "Why can't we see that other tulip garden that you say is just up there over this one?"

"We can try," Kay answered. "But it takes a special kind of looking to see it, doesn't it, Nan?"

"How shall we look then?"

"I don't know exactly."

"But Gentian went there through the walls of Nan's attic room, you told me. How did you do that, Gentian?"

"By getting deep-still."

"What is that?"

Gentian could not explain.

Now Nan, who had been lying on her back nibbling a sweet grass blade, said, "There are many, many ways of looking to see into the Clear Land. Let's lie quietly on our backs here for a little and just try."

So the four playmates lay on their backs in the cool grass and tried to see up into the Clear Land. But for all their looking, and all their expectant stillness, it did not take shape for them in the blue spring air.

Rosemarie was the first to grow impatient. She sat up. "Oh, there is nothing but blue sky up there," she cried, "and white clouds. I think it must have been all your imagining, Kay and Gentian!"

"No, no!" Kay protested. "It was no imagining. You ought to see the statuette Mother has made of the Wind Boy. Then you'd know he was as real as you are!"

"Oh, has your mother seen him too?"

"Yes, of course. But the funny thing about that is that she does not remember she has!"

"I should think that *was* a funny thing. Too funny to be true. I don't—"

"Oh, but it is just as Kay tells you," Nan interrupted. She was still stretched on her back, looking up into the blue spring air. "The truest and most important things are almost always those we have no words for. That is what Kay means by not remembering—his mother doesn't tell it over to herself in words when she gets back from the Clear Land. But she tells it in other ways—like the Wind Boy statue—and it's in her eyes. Wait till you see her, Rosemarie!"

Although Nan said this, and it explained nothing to Rosemarie, still she at once believed her, and laughed no more.

"Let's go and see the statuette," Gentian suggested then. "You will love it, Rosemarie, just as we do."

"All right. Only not for a little while. It's so cool and comfortable here in the grass, and I'm finding such funny pictures in the clouds. Wait a little."

"I will go and bring the statuette here instead," Nan said, getting up suddenly. "It will be all the more beautiful, out here with the sun on it."

Now, neither Kay nor Gentian would have thought of touching their mother's work. But it never entered their heads that Nan was doing anything wrong. And they were right to believe in her so.

She ran away to fetch the statuette.

Rosemarie, who was sitting up, watched her go. "Running, she looks just like a relief of a dancing girl on an old Greek vase in Grandfather's study," she said. "She moves as though she were hearing music!"

"Yes, she walks like that too; I've often noticed," Kay agreed thoughtfully. "Sometimes I almost hear it too—the music. But never quite."

After that they lay quiet, saying no more, until Nan returned with the statuette held very carefully before her. She stood it up in their midst in the grassy place.

Rosemarie knelt in front of it. "Oh, he is just as you described him, Kay," she cried. "And he is shining, too. You didn't describe that!"

"I have been wondering about that shining," Kay said. "When he's just made out of gray plastilina, where does the shiningness come from?"

"Why, that's his happiness," Nan tried to explain. "It shines out through his face, and even through his wings and body."

"But the statuette can't be happy. It's only a statuette!"

"That is true. But your mother could copy the happiness, and here it is."

"I wonder," Gentian said suddenly and softly, "I wonder if that is what the Clear Land is—happiness. And this land down here is only the copy of that shining? Even ourselves only copies?"

"Oh, Gentian," Nan said, "perhaps. You must ask the Great Artist up there sometime. I don't know."

Rosemarie was still kneeling in front of the statuette. It was so alive-seeming, she almost expected at any minute that the breeze would stir in its curls, and its wings bend. As the minutes passed, and it still remained, always ready for flight but never flying, her strange surprise grew. That will tell you how real and beautiful Detra had made him.

They were all so absorbed, Gentian in her new, searching thoughts, Rosemarie in the statuette, Kay in Rosemarie's delight, and Nan in them all, that they did not hear the Artist coming down the path toward them. For some time he stood, all unknown, above them. But after a while he spoke.

"What is that?" his voice rang with wonder and delight. "Who brought this beautiful thing here?"

"I did," Nan answered, no surprise in her face, as she turned to him.

"Is it yours?"

"No. It is Detra's. She made it last night. She did not go to bed at all."

"I should think not! Who is Detra?"

"Why, she is our mother," both Kay and Gentian cried together, proudly.

"Why have I not known?" Then: "May I take it up?" he asked of Nan.

You may think it strange that the great Artist should ask of Nan, the general housework girl, permission to touch a statuette he had found being played with by the children in his garden. But if you think so, that is because you have not seen the statuette, and you have not seen Nan!

"Yes," she nodded. "Detra would like you to see it."

Very gently, even reverently, the Artist raised the little statuette up and held it out before him in the afternoon sunlight. He turned it around and around slowly, his eyes narrow and intent, as Detra's eyes had been narrow and intent when she worked on it.

"Is she at home now, the artist?" he asked finally.

He spoke of Detra as the "artist"! The children's eyes shone.

"No, she is at the factory," Nan answered. "She works there all day. But she will come soon now."

"In a factory! The creator of this! Working in a factory!"

"Yes, they are refugees. The father who went to the war

has lost track of them. So Detra cannot stay at home with her children. She must earn bread and a roof for their heads, in a factory."

"She shall never go there again, if I can help it. May I take this to her house for its safety, and wait there for her?"

Nan nodded. "She will be glad of your praise," she said.

"But she must have more than praise," the Artist thought to himself. "She must be paid for this, if she will let me have it. It shall be done into bronze, and stand here just where I found it, beside a fountain. Here in the tulip garden the Wind Boy will stand always on tiptoe, about to fly. People will come far to see it."

At that Gentian clapped her hands. It was a soft clapping, but the Artist heard and turned to look down at her. He said, smiling now for the first time, "You were right all the time, little Wind Girl, when you assured me that the Wind Boy was real. Your mother has proved for us forever that he is real, real as ourselves!"

Detra was very, very tired when she came home from the factory that evening. She had not been to bed at all the night before, you will remember. But when she turned in at her little gate, she braced her body, put back her shoulders, and made her steps light to greet her children. She came in with a high head, and her eyes smiling.

But she stopped, amazed, in the door. For there, rising to meet her, was the Artist, his head, topped with its mass of gray curls, just escaping the low ceiling of the little room. In his hand he still held carefully the Wind Boy. He could not let it go.

"Good evening," said Detra.

"Good evening," answered the Artist.

Detra untied her cape at the neck and dropped it beside her onto a chair. In the cape, and in the shadow of the room, she looked like a tired working woman. But now, without the dark garment, and in the light of the candles that Nan had just brought in, she was *herself*, the self the children always saw. Her wide, frank eyes, her high-held head, her straight slim body, made her look like a brighter, and human, candle.

The Artist bowed his head over the statuette. "This is beauty," he said.

"Yes, I know," Detra replied, tranquilly. "I saw so clearly last night that I stayed up all night to work."

"I want to buy it of you, for my tulip garden."

And then Detra and the Artist sat down on the bench under the window and talked. Nan was getting supper, and setting the table. But it did not interrupt the artists, for she passed back and forth as softly as a shadow. Outside the door, under the cherry tree, Kay and Gentian and Rosemarie had gone to play. But the sound of their laughter did not disturb the Artist and Detra.

When you have created a beautiful thing, that is happiness. But the next happiness is to find someone who understands what you have done, and knows that it is beautiful. Detra had both.

But at last supper was ready, and the children came in. Rosemarie stood by her grandfather. He got up.

"I shall share this with the artists of the world," he said. "Tomorrow all the papers shall have news of your genius and its promise. Then your husband, if only he is alive and searching, must come upon your name, and find you."

"I have been thinking of that all the time you were talking," Detra answered. "And if he does find us now, we shall take this money you are paying for the Wind Boy and buy the meadows behind this house, and he will turn them into tree nurseries. At home, before the war, that was what my husband did. Fruit trees. He is marvelous at it. Then we shall live on here in our adopted country, for there is nothing left in the old for us."

The Artist nodded, well pleased with the plan. "I shall send my wires and cables at once," he promised. "Tomorrow the world will know that here in this little brown house lives a new, great artist. If your husband is alive, there's a chance he'll hear of it, or read it."

That night the little brown house, set like a stepping stone to the Artist's great one, could scarcely hold its happiness. At last the three had reason to hope that Hazar would find them! Soon. The Artist had been so sure. They had had no one to help them before.

But Gentian awoke in the night to remember the Wind Boy. He had said he liked her best. He had kissed her. He had been a perfect playmate. But now he had forgotten, and was staying away in the Clear Land with the Clear Children.

In spite of all her happiness, Gentian's blue eyes in the dark were touched with puzzled wonder.

Chapter 18

Comrades

THE Artist was true to his word. While the family in the little brown cottage slept, the telegraph wires and the radio waves and even the great cables under the oceans were busy with the news: our greatest living Artist has discovered a genius, a new and entirely unknown sculptress. He has bought a statuette from her and paid a fabulous sum for it. She is a refugee living with her children at his very door, and has lived there for a year without his knowing about her work. Then came her full name, and her story.

By morning all the papers in the country had the story, and many printed it in headlines on their front pages.

The people living in the Artist's village could hardly believe their eyes when they read. Their surprise and excitement were immense. Why, they had seen Detra every morning going to work in her dark cape! There had been no sign about her of this; or if there had been a sign, they had failed to see it.

Their curiosity led some of them, even so early in the morning, to go out and walk down the street to take a good look at the little brown cottage that now housed so much fame. There was even pride in their gaze, for after all Detra was one of them, one of their village!

And when Kay and Gentian, with Rosemarie, ran by on their way to school, the villagers looked after them, thoughtfully.

"Well, things will be different for those children after this," they said wisely, nodding their heads at one another. "And it's a good thing. For better-mannered or brighter children you would go far to find."

As for Detra, she went to her work that morning as usual. For she meant to tell her employer about her good fortune, and give him a fair chance to replace her. But her feet, today, went lightly toward her task and she walked like a queen—not as a proud queen, you must know, but as a happy one. For she had a strong hope that somehow, somewhere, Hazar, the children's father, would read the news, and so find them at last.

And it did happen just as she hoped. In a city not far away, that very morning, a man with copper-colored hair and eyes blue as the sea stopped at a corner to read the headlines of the newspapers displayed there on a stand. And immediately the name Detra shone out for him in rainbow lettering! It was his joy that made the lettering rainbow, of course, for it was just in printer's ink for ordinary eyes. From that minute, that copper-haired young man moved as in a cloud.

For that young man was Hazar, the children's father. He had traced his wife and his children to this country directly after the war, and since then he had been wandering from city to city, seeking them.

But he thought little about the jobs, for his real work was his searching. His eyes were always searching, searching among crowds in all the poorer sections of the cities. And he would stand outside of stores and factories at the close of the working day, hoping that Detra might come out of some dark door and see him waiting there!

And then at noon hour he would wait in the same way at the doors of school buildings. His blue eyes had grown haggard watching at school doors for two little coppery heads.

But now that was ended. He was a young god striding away out of the city toward the road that led to the Artist's village. People who had never given him a glance before, in his shabby workman's clothes and with his haggard, seeking eyes, now turned to stare after him as he passed.

But though it would not have taken him long by train, it was long to walk, and Hazar was a day and a night in coming to the village.

That day Nan had spent in making the little brown house spick-and-span from top to bottom; for although she had not yet told Detra, she knew that her work here was finished. The mountains were calling her back.

Kay and Gentian, in school at their desks, and playing at recess time, and all the afternoon as they played with Rosemarie in her grandfather's gardens, often lifted their heads to listen, for they thought they heard their father calling their names!

When bedtime came again, Detra and the children and even Nan slept but fitfully, they were so alive with their expectation. And all during breakfast the children talked of nothing but their father.

"Will he come today? Do you think he might come today?"

But Detra, whose heart was beating even faster than her children's, said, "No, no. Hush! We must not expect him so soon. Why, he may be across the ocean, across the world from us!"

But in spite of those sensible words, at every step that came down the street, she turned her head to listen! Would it turn in at the little swinging gate? And the children listened with her.

Detra's employer had found someone at once to take Detra's place, and so she was to be at home, today, all day, and every day. That was glorious for the children.

But the glory faded, vanished for a little while, when Nan, after she had done the dishes and put the house in order, went up to her room, and came down with her knotted purple bundle. Detra looked at her in surprise.

"Why Nan, you're not going to go away from us! Not *now!*"

Nan nodded. "There is nothing left here for me to do," she said. "I cannot stay where there is no work."

Detra got up from the bench under the window, where she had been sitting arranging fresh tulips in the bowl. She looked at Nan earnestly and steadily.

She did not say, "But there *is* work, Nan! The house to keep clean, meals to cook, dishes to wash. Please stay on to do these things for us."

No, it did not enter Detra's head to utter such foolishness. For Detra, now for the first time, began to understand about Nan, and what she might be. That had not been the work she had left her mountains to do. She had come to help Detra toward happiness. And now Detra was happy, and all was well with her and the children.

So Detra said not a word, but stood looking at Nan steadily.

But the children were dismayed. They cried, "Oh, please, please, Nan, don't go away and leave us! You must never do that!"

Nan turned to them, smiling. "Why, unless I go back to the mountains, then how can you come to visit me there? And that is what I want you to do. Soon!"

Their hearts were eased.

Detra at last said, "Are you a good fairy, Nan? Is that what you are?"

"No, I am not a fairy." But she answered gravely, as though in reply to a sensible question—as though she might very well have been a fairy, only it happened that she was not. "I am just a girl from the mountains."

Detra asked no more, and Nan moved toward the door. Kay and Gentian heard the music that she walked to then. There could be no doubt about it this time, though it was faint and far.

Gentian ran after her. "Oh, may I have one last peep at the starry-brightness?" she begged.

Nan held the purple bundle to her. Gentian parted the sides a little, and looked in. Yes, there was the blue, shining with its stars. Gentian bent above the purple bundle, looking into the sky. If she had not remembered her own bit of sky folded away upstairs in her drawer, she could never have had done with looking now.

When she lifted her face, her eyes had caught the reflection of the stars.

Nan tied her bundle a little tighter then, so that no one as she passed along the street might catch a glimpse of the stars or suspect what wonderful thing was tied away there. Then she said good-by.

The children clung to her as far as the gate, and stood watching there while she went away down the street. But they could not be unhappy over her going. For this thing was true about Nan—no one could ever be unhappy because of her! But they stayed swinging on the gate, silent and thoughtful, after she had gone around the corner.

A little way around the corner, as Nan walked to the sound of that music, faint and far, she met a young man.

He was striding along with the morning sun in his eyes. His hair was a flame of copper.

Nan could not help knowing at once that it was the children's father, Hazar, nearing the end of his search. She spoke to him, coming to a stand before him on the sidewalk. But his eyes were full of the morning sun, rather blinded; and to him it seemed that it was only a voice in the street, speaking to him out of the sunlight. He could never remember afterwards having seen Nan. But he remembered her words.

"If you are looking for Detra's little brown cottage, it is just around that corner. And Gentian and Kay are out in front, swinging on the gate."

The young man did not even thank her, for you see he never realized, until afterwards when the children told him so, that a young girl must have given him the direction. He truly thought it was only a voice out of the sunshine, the morning sunshine that was full in his eyes. But he heard the words well enough.

And suddenly he started running. He ran around the corner as fast as his long legs would take him. And the next minute, both the children on the gate had uttered shrill glad cries that brought Detra to the door.

When she got there, she saw Hazar with Gentian and Kay tight in his arms, as though he would never let them go.

Then Detra cried out too, and ran down the walk. But Hazar was quicker than she. He let the children go and met her halfway from the door.

The Artist, at that minute, was coming through the hole

in the hedge. He had had it made larger, for his convenience, the day before. He was coming for a morning call. But he stopped short when he saw Hazar and Detra meeting. And the morning sunshine got into his eyes, or something did, for he saw no more, but turned away, and waited until later for his visit to the little brown house.

That was a marvelous day for Kay and Gentian. They held to their father's hands, leaned against him whenever he stood still, and followed him about like shadows. Most of the morning they wandered over the meadows at the back of the house while their father and mother talked about the young tree nurseries that he was to grow there. The children were so happy they were unusually quiet.

As for Detra, they looked at her wonderingly again and again. For she did not seem like their mother at all now. She was like a wide-eyed young girl listening to a fairy tale. They had all forgotten about school, of course. But no one ever blamed them for that!

In the afternoon Hazar and Detra took a bench out under the cherry tree. The children sat at their feet in the grass. It was then that they noticed the Policeman walking back and forth, pausing irresolutely each time as he reached the gate, almost as though he would put it open and come in.

About the twentieth time this happened, Hazar called to him: "Do you want anything, Officer?"

At that the Policeman took courage and did push the gate open.

"It's welcome you are to this village," he said to Hazar, for he knew very well who he was, and he meant his welcome heartily. But then he turned to Detra and asked in a hesitating voice, "Has your girl left you? I saw her on the street with a bundle this morning. She looked almost as if she was going away."

"She has. She's gone back to the mountains," Detra told him.

The children saw how sorry the Policeman was to hear this, and they felt sorry for him.

"Well, with a man in the house now, and all, I suppose

the work might very well be too hard for a slip of a girl like that!" they heard him mutter.

"No indeed," Detra answered, laughing. She had not noticed his sorriness. "It was just because the work was too easy that she left us. She thought she could no longer find enough to do. She said so."

The Policeman shook his head. He could not understand that at all. He asked, "Then will you kindly let me have her address? I might be taking a trip to the mountains some day."

Her address! Detra and the children looked at one another in sudden bewilderment. How could they ever have neglected to ask Nan for that! Just "Nan, the Mountains," was no address, Detra had to admit.

The Policeman stared. "Don't you know at all where she's gone to?" he asked.

"Only that she's gone back to the mountains."

"Which mountains?"

"Why, I see now that I don't know that. But I always supposed the purple mountains—the ones we see off there, beyond the meadows and the wood."

"Yes, that's what I thought, too," the Policeman muttered. "But that isn't enough to find her by. And there was something quite particular I had to say to her!"

Gentian suddenly stood up and took the man's hand. Yes, Gentian took the Policeman's hand, the big hand that had gripped Kay by the shoulder so recently. She said softly but surely, her blue eyes looking confidently up into his, "She promised that Kay and I were to go to the mountains

to visit her. Soon! That means she will let us know where
she lives when the time comes. And we can tell you."

The Policeman in some strange, deep way was comforted.
It was as though Nan herself had reassured him, through
Gentian's voice!

And so he turned back to his tramping of the peaceful
village streets, with his puzzlements changed into thought-
fulness.

When the Policeman had gone, the Artist came through
the hole in the hedge. Then he and Hazar and Detra put
their heads together in a very grown-up way to make plans
for the future of Detra's art, and Hazar's tree nurseries.

The children lost interest at that. And they were glad to
hear Rosemarie calling them, although they had heard her
before that afternoon without answering. She was playing
with some of their schoolmates on the Artist's lawn. The
lawn was a sea, and the sundial was a pirate ship. Rosemarie
was the captain.

"Come along, Kay and Gentian," she called. "We're on
the track of hidden treasure."

So Kay left his father's side and ran away to be a pirate.
But Gentian got no farther than the door. There she suddenly had no heart for play, and sat down on the door stone.

"Aren't you coming?" Kay called back to her in surprise
from over the hedge.

"By and by I'll come, perhaps—not now."

So the pirates went dashing off after hidden treasure

without her. Now she could think the thought that had been knocking at the door of her mind through the day, under all the happiness of her father's return. It was, "It isn't fair that the Wind Boy should stay away so. I wouldn't give him up for Kay and all those others. But he gave me up the minute he got his Clear Comrades back again."

After a time the Artist came out of the door to go home. But he stopped for a minute by Gentian to say, "Why aren't you off with Kay and Rosemarie, little Wind Girl? Or are you waiting here for your Wind Boy?"

"No, I'm not waiting for him," Gentian answered, looking up rather mournfully at the Artist. "He doesn't come to play any more."

The Artist looked rueful. "Is that because I have taken him away for a while? But soon he will be back, you know, all done into bronze, life-sized, and out in the tulip garden. He will play with you then, won't he?"

"No. I didn't mean the statue! I mean the real Wind Boy up in the Clear Village. The one Mother copied. It's him I've lost."

"I'm sorry," the Artist said to that. "But perhaps his wings will bring him back down to you yet. Who knows?" The Artist was so fond of his little "Wind Girl" already that it troubled him to see her sad.

When he had gone, Gentian suddenly thought, "Well, anyway I have my starry-brightness. I can run up and see that." And she did get up and go softly into the house.

Through the open sitting-room door she saw her mother and father sitting on the bench under the window. They were looking at each other, saying nothing, but smiling. Gentian went past on tiptoe. "They are glad to be alone," she thought.

When she got up to her mother's room and had opened her own bottom drawer, she knelt before it on the floor, looking deep, deep into the starry blue depths.

And as she looked, her thoughts cleared. They cleared until they were crystal clear. And this is what came into their clearness:

"How foolish I am! Of course the Wind Boy will come back. He is my comrade. He wouldn't forget me, just because he was happy. He would remember all the more. He would remember *all the more.*"

She was herself again. Light-heartedly she closed the drawer and jumped up. "I'll just go and play pirate after all," she thought. "Perhaps, while we're playing, the Wind Boy will come. Sometime, anyway!"

But now that she was standing, she saw that she was through into the Clear Land! The light was not sunlight any more, but the crystal, clearer light of the higher village. And again she was alone in a room of the house belonging to the Twilight Girl. She looked toward the window.

There were the cherry-tree boughs, all in flower with pink and white blossoms. Not the boughs of the cherry tree that stood at the door of the little brown house, but the boughs of the other cherry tree above it in the Clear Air!

The cherry blossoms down there were still in bud, but these up here were full blown.

And there among the cherry blossoms, on a swaying bough, waited the Wind Boy. She knew he was waiting by the droop of his wings, and the expression of his face. But it was not the Wind Boy as she had seen him first. Now the light across his brow was clear. He was wearing silver sandals like her own.

He did not see her standing at the window. He was looking down through the blossoming branches, as though he expected her to come up that way.

"Oh, Wind Boy!" she called. "Here I am. I have come!"

He started up, looking about. Laughing, she jumped over the window sill and went running to him through the blue air.

The Wind Boy made room for her, balancing on the trembling bough. "It took you long enough," he said, holding her hands. "It's been two whole days!"

"Oh, but I was looking for you all that time down in our village. You see, I don't know how to get up here. My coming just has to happen. I can do nothing about it. But you could come down to me, any time!"

"And I did go down, of course. Many, many times! But I couldn't get you to see me."

"Not see you! I was looking for you every minute. Even today with Father there!"

"Yes, you were looking for me. But were you believing in me?"

"Believing in you? Of course. Why, I've always known you were real as real—no matter how much anyone calls you a dream!"

"Oh, *that* kind of real, yes! That is nothing. You couldn't help knowing that, could you? I mean, were you believing in the *real* myself, the comrading part of me?"

Gentian dropped her head. "No, that is what I had stopped believing in," she owned. "I had stopped believing that you were my comrade. I thought you wanted only your Clear Children playmates now."

The Wind Boy smiled.

"Well, that tells us, then, why you had to come up here to find me. I could never have got to you there with such silly thoughts in your head. But you've come at last. And it's all right. We are comrades."

"Where are the Clear Children?" Gentian asked then. "Why are you alone?"

"I was only waiting for you. They are over in the wood by the spring, looking for flowers. We'll go find them.—But you've never been to the spring, have you? There are little gray stones in the bottom. They are gray when you first look, but after a while—"

"Yes, I know. Then they are all-color."

"Oh, you have been there!" The Wind Boy sounded disappointed that he was not to be the first to show her.

"No. I do not think I was there. But I saw you there. You were with my mother. She was working on the statuette all the time she was talking to you. She was trying to make you smile."

"Yes. She was telling me stories, stories you had told her, she said. But where were you? Why didn't we know you were near?"

"I was only looking through the spring, the one below. Neither you nor Mother could see me, nor hear me when I called. And I could not hear your words either, though I saw your lips moving."

The Wind Boy shuddered. "That must have been horrid. Strange and horrid!"

"Yes, it was."

"Well, it's nothing like that this time. You're here now, safe and sound in the Clear Land. Aziel will be waiting by the spring to see if you came. She thought you would surely find the way."

"Aziel? Oh, I'm glad! Come, let's go."Gentian and the Wind Boy ran away fleetly then, out paths of blue air toward the Clear Spring in the Clear Woods. And the Wind Boy spread his wings so wide as they went, that I lost sight of Gentian behind their purple.